The Void

Entangled Series
Book 8

Jill Sanders

GRAYTON

Summary

Mia has always been aware of the things that lurk in the darkness. The weight of her family's age-old obligations has molded her entire life. Now she's trapped in a lost world and confronted by the very things that terrify most people. This time, things have changed. The balance has shifted and, if she can't break free, she just might find herself consumed by the darkness.

Lucas has returned to the Void to save Mia, but without his own special abilities, he's powerless to help her. The journey to reach her is treacherous, but it's nothing compared to the fight they have ahead. As they ready for the coming battle against evil, they must confront not only the darkness that threatens to destroy this realm but also the feelings that are growing between them.

Can Lucas find a way to save Mia before the darkness destroys her world? And will their love be enough to overcome the challenges they face?

Prologue

Six-year-old Mia Li stood next to her one-hundred-and-two-year-old great-uncle Bai, who was lying on a large slab of stone in the middle of the cavern. Her uncle's small body—almost as small as hers—was covered in soft blue silk. She wore a dress made of matching silk.

The dress was far too long for her short legs, and the arms covered her fingertips. Her mother and aunt had made the dress specifically for tonight, so why had they made it so big?

She'd worn traditional clothing before. After all, for each New Year celebration, her entire family dressed up and enjoyed the fun.

This dress was different, though. Something her family had called Hanfu.

Mia's long jet-black hair was tied up in a tight bun on the top of her head. Beads lined her face. Her mother had even let her wear a pearl necklace and earrings for the occasion.

Mia felt pretty, but she was annoyed that she couldn't

play in the dress, or even walk without almost falling over, for that matter.

Every single member of her family surrounded her and her uncle. All forty-some of them. Of course, she knew them all by name. She'd grown up seeing them often.

She knew that it should have been Lei standing in the circle instead of her. Her older brother had died four years before in a tragic accident when he'd been five. She and her parents never talked about him or what had happened to him. Honestly, she had been too young back then to really remember him much. What she did remember was how kind he'd been to her, how good he'd been. He'd been her very first best friend.

Lei had been the one born for this burden. He'd been the one preparing to take on this task when needed. Now, that responsibility fell to her.

Since that day when Lei left her life, she'd been schooled on what would one day happen. The day she was to receive the great gift of her family. Today was that day, yet she still felt unprepared.

Her family was singing softly in unison in their native tongue, a dialect of old Mandarin. Their chants were so hypnotic that she lost herself in the music. She'd known the words to the ancient song her entire life. She wanted to join in the chorus, but suddenly, her little body was frozen in place.

She wanted to scream, to call out to her Ma and Ba, but nothing on her seemed to work anymore. Her body simply refused to obey her.

Then she was lifted high up in the air as everyone around her watched. No one seemed surprised or scared, and she relaxed slightly.

The Void

After she was lifted almost twenty feet off the ground, a bright blue light slowly drifted from her uncle's chest. When it started moving towards her, she felt tears sting her eyes. What did it want with her? Was it her uncle's soul? Was he going to take over her body?

When the sphere slid effortlessly into her own chest, a burst of knowledge flooded her young mind.

Every fiber of her being was melted together with every member of her family who had ever carried the same gift over the centuries. Hundreds of centuries. Thousands and thousands of family member's voices flooded her young mind in those precious seconds.

Images, sharp and vivid, flashed behind her eyes. In mere seconds, she lived a thousand different lives. Loved a thousand different lovers. Died a thousand different ways.

When she did finally scream, her body jerked in the air. Her fingers and toes reached out for something to hold onto as pain, red hot, seared through every fiber of her being.

The voice of every Li family member who had possessed the gift screamed in her mind all at once. Moments past and suddenly the sounds subsided until they were nothing more than whispers.

When her feet finally landed softly on the ground, Mia was no longer just a six-year-old girl. She was djinn.

Glancing over, she looked at the shell of her great-uncle, who had willingly passed on his gift to her. She walked over and touched his frail cheek while he looked up at her through unseeing eyes. As the first tear slid down her cheek, she whispered, "Rest." Then she watched as every atom in his body shattered and separated, floated up into the air, and disappeared into the darkness.

Her parents rushed to hug her. To comfort her. Only

she didn't need consoling. She had thousands of voices in her head. Countless memories of the past to relive in her mind. The knowledge of thousands of her ancestors, other djinns, would keep her company now.

She no longer needed anyone else.

Chapter One

Twenty years later...

She was in deep shit. There was no way she was going to get out of this new situation alone.

Where was Selene? Lucas? Scott? Any of her new friends.

One minute they'd been standing at the base of the gates of hell, talking to the three fates: Clotho, Spinner of life, Lachesis, dispenser of life, and Atropos, ender of life.

She, Lucas, Selene, and Scott had gone to the Beyond, as Selene had called it, which was basically hell, to find a way to bind Moros, the god of doom. He, apparently, was on the verge of destroying everything. All worlds. All realms.

After she had run into Selene in her apartment complex and felt the woman's power, she'd known instantly that their fates were intertwined So she'd invited Selene and Scott to her family's home just outside of Atlanta in order to train for the doom that Selene warned was coming.

Her friendship with Selene and Scott had progressed quickly. They didn't judge her, and early on she realized they weren't going to use her either.

Then Selene's brother showed up unexpectedly.

The first time she met Lucas Romano, aka the reincarnation of Helios, the sun god, he was nothing like she'd imaged after hearing Selene describe her brother. Instead of an ugly, dark sinister-looking villain, the man was more like a mysterious sexy god. He had been dressed in very expensive clothing and had his jet-black hair cut short around the sides and longer on top. His amber eyes were mesmerizing. Whenever he looked at her, she felt her insides shake with want.

When she'd stood in the kitchen that first night after he'd shown up at her parents' place, she'd had a difficult time focusing.

"As I've mentioned to Selene, I'm in need of your assistance," Lucas had said, his eyes moving to her once more. Since his arrival, he'd been trying to assess her. She'd instantly felt his power and wondered if he could feel hers. "What exactly are you?" he asked, finally.

"Your worst nightmare if you cause problems," she'd blurted out. And she had meant it. She had instantly known she was more powerful than him. Since Selene had been unsure of Lucas's intentions at that point, she'd wanted to make sure where he stood.

For the first time since Selene had shown her brother into the house, Lucas smiled. And when he did, Mia's legs turned to jelly. Shit. This wasn't good. There was no way just seeing a man smile should make her this weak.

"Interesting," Lucas said slowly, turning away to give her a chance to recover.

For a few moments, they'd talked about Scott's powers being hidden. Mia had always thought the man, who had lived in her building, was hiding something. Not once had she believed it was anything she needed

The Void

to be aware of. Still, she'd watched him over the past year.

Mia was surprised when, to showcase his abilities, Lucas stood up from the barstool and turned into a large black dog right in front of them. It was so huge, its fur nearly touched the ceiling.

"Mia can do that too," Selene broke in, and Lucas's yellow dog eyes turned towards her.

"Show me," Lucas, or rather the dog, said firmly.

Mia set down the mug of coffee she was holding, took a deep breath, and shifted into her dog form. She was much smaller than Lucas was and, to be honest, less scary looking. Standing next to him, she felt like a poodle comparing herself to a dire wolf.

They both stared at one another for a moment before turning back into themselves.

"Don't your clothes get ripped off?" Scott had asked when they were done. Mia had wanted to laugh, but the truth was, the first time she'd shifted, she'd wondered about that too. It had been years before she realized why they didn't. When she changed, whatever she was wearing or had on her changed too. Her clothes became fur. If she had a bag on, it became a collar. Scott cleared his throat. "I mean, you just shifted into furry dogs."

"Hellhounds," Lucas corrected.

"Seriously?" Mia practically barked back. "I've always thought of myself more as a dog," she admitted with a smile.

The corner of Lucas's lips curved up again, and she had to lean against the railing to steady herself.

"It takes three of us," Lucas said to the room. "Now I know who the third is." He nodded to her.

"So I am needed." She smiled as she picked up the mug again.

"And Selene is our ticket to hell," Lucas said.

"So, what? I'm just supposed to deliver the three of you to the Beyond," Selene had asked, "and watch you wake up the devil?"

"Not the devil. Well, in a sense. I mean..." Lucas actually looked irritated or... embarrassed. "Yes, his name is Hades, but no, he's not the devil in Western mythology or religion. Think of him as... the gatekeeper to the destruction of everything."

"Then why wake him?" Scott had asked.

"Because there is a rip in the gates. A leak. One that only he can mend," Lucas explained.

"Okay, so..." Mia leaned on the counter. "Hades is a good guy?"

"Yes and no. Once we wake him, we will need to get out of there quickly. Selene will deliver us three, we will wake him, then change into..." He motioned with his hands.

"Hellhounds," Mia had supplied.

"And let Hades find and fix the leak," Lucas explained.

"How do you know there's a leak?" Selene had asked.

"Because that is how our parents escaped," Lucas said.

Hearing the gravity of the situation had caused Mia some concern. But her heart had skipped whenever she saw Lucas or trained with him over the next few weeks.

How many other men had caused her body to instantly react in her life? None. So she'd done what she could to keep him at arm's length. She was afraid to get too close to anyone outside of her family for fear they would judge or use her.

Mia had learned to live with her gifts with help from her family. For the first ten years of her new life with her powers, she'd remained at her family's secluded home just outside of Atlanta and had trained every day, learning all

The Void

about the djinn's history and all the myths surrounding them.

On her sixteenth birthday, she and her parents moved back to the city. She attended school for the first time in her life. It was a private school, but she'd finally been around other kids her own age.

Because of her family's gift, and the knowledge of said gift, the Lis, all of them, were very wealthy. Each member that passed on assured that wealth was kept within the family.

It wasn't often that a family knew exactly where they had come from more than ten millennia ago.

The Lis had come from Kòngbái, or as Mia had started calling it, the Void. It was a planet—or a realm, depending on which family member you were talking to—far, far away. The place sat empty now, destitute, void of everything.

Once, long ago, before the Li family had traveled to Earth, Kòngbái, had been thriving with life. There had been large cities, technology, and even some sort of space travel, which had been recorded in the archives that her family kept in their private vault. It was housed in a massive underground cavern on the other world, safe from any prying eyes on Earth.

Each year, on the anniversary of the reckoning, the day she'd come into the djinn powers, she would travel with the elders to the cave. There, each of them would read through the family's histories in search of... well, at this point, she didn't know. Maybe they were just reading for pleasure?

She'd always grown bored on these travels. At first, when she was still a child, she had enjoyed the few hours of downtime from her studies. When she'd grown older, she'd just found the old dusty cavern tedious.

She was forced to be there since only djinns had the

power to go between realms or worlds. It was her duty to keep up the traditions.

It was also her duty as djinn to help others in their fight to save humanity. And that is how she had found herself standing at the gates of hell with her new friends in the first place.

The massive gates had been spectacular and extremely scary. They stood more than a hundred stories high with black spikes on either side of the opening. They had been more impressive than anything Mia had ever laid eyes on in her lifetime, either on Earth or in the Void.

Along each spike, snake-like creatures twisted and turned, opening and closing the gates as the shadows of souls passed through them silently.

Seeing that had caused a shiver to race through her. She hadn't feared death since witnessing her uncle's all those years ago. He'd passed peacefully and, in a way, still willingly lived within her, all in order to pass the family gift to her. As she would do one day in the very distant future.

So when the three witches, or fates, had zapped her back to the Void against her will, at first she'd shrugged it off. At least she could return home. Hopefully, Scott, Lucas, and Selene had gotten the rest of the information they needed about how to fight Moros and win.

But when she had tried to return to her family's home, nothing happened.

Now she stood in the middle of the desert on the Void—Kòngbái—the home of her ancestors, alone and stranded.

It wasn't until she started walking that she realized she was no longer wearing the worn jeans, sweatshirt, and tennis shoes that she'd been wearing when they'd left her family home in Georgia to travel to hell.

Instead, she was wearing the same soft blue silk dress

she'd worn as a child. Now, however, the dress seemed to fit her perfectly.

It wasn't the first time she'd appeared in the dress here. When she traveled to this realm alone, she remained in her own clothes. But when she brought her family members on their yearly trip, she appeared in this same dress.

Why was she wearing it now?

Why couldn't she return home?

Glancing around, she groaned at the two bright yellow suns hanging high in the sky. If she was stuck here, the first thing she'd have to do is find water or shelter.

Mountains surrounded the desert on all sides of the sand like a ring, circling it like a protective barrier, as if the flat sand was being held in place by the higher peaks.

In the hundreds of times she'd been here, she'd never once traveled beyond the sand. The family cavern was somewhere high up in the mountains, but when she'd needed to travel there, she and her family members always appeared directly inside the cave.

If she'd lost her ability to return to Earth, had all her other powers gone too?

She closed her eyes and concentrated. When she looked down at her hands, she smiled at the furry black paws that sank into the hot sand.

Okay, so she could still shift into a dog. Check that off the list.

What about her other gifts?

She didn't have as many as some of her ancestors had. The numerous powers the Li family djinn had boasted were an enigma to her.

She'd been stuck with shapeshifting, stopping time, and traveling to the Void. She could also travel to a place she called the Between, a space where no one could get hurt and time moved differently. Then there was her gift of giving visions. It was like Selene's power of giving waking nightmares to all who touched her, but Mia's visions were, well, good.

Mia couldn't keep her dog form for too long, so she turned back into her regular form and started walking towards the mountains. How far were they, anyway?

Why had she never dared to travel on foot to them before? Sure, she'd appeared in her family's cavern, which was hidden somewhere within those mountains, but she'd never explored beyond the sand or the cavern.

Something in her mind screamed for her to stop. To not go there. But she was hot, thirsty, and tired.

The two suns above her beat down on her, and she pulled off the dress's long sleeves and bulky over-jacket before she overheated.

She'd never been in the Void longer than a few hours and had never spent more than a few moments in the desert. Usually, she only traveled there for a moment of peace and quiet.

Stopping, she closed her eyes and silently wished for a bottled water. She gasped when she felt one appear in her hand. She opened her eyes and smiled. She quickly tore off the lid and drank down every last drop.

If she could conjure a bottled water, what else could she do? She tried a few different things, but got frustrated when nothing else seemed to work.

After almost two hours of walking and not feeling she was any closer to the mountain range, she sat in the sand, frustrated.

What she needed was shade. She groaned and threw a handful of sand in the direction that she'd been traveling.

Suddenly, the sand a few feet away from her shifted and

The Void

started to swirl. She jumped up and backed away a few feet, watching in amazement as a tall monolith rose slowly from the sand, twisting until it hovered over her almost a hundred feet.

When the sand around it stopped moving, she cautiously approached the tower. There, in the base of the solid stone, was an arched doorway made of wood. A large symbol was carved in the thick wood.

Down the middle was a large slash. On either side, two triangles were turned on their sides, their points crossing.

The symbol was beautiful... and somehow familiar.

Reaching out, she touched it with her fingers, tracing the line down the center. Suddenly, a blue light flashed and the door slowly opened.

She took a few steps back and then peered into the darkness.

Nothing like this had ever happened to her before.

"Welcome, Mia," a soothing female voice called out to her. "Please, you are safe here."

She stepped inside the door. The moment she was in the darkness, the door slammed shut, sending the room into complete darkness.

"I've been waiting for you," the female voice said.

Suddenly, a light shone on a table that was filled with small plates of colorful food and a pitcher of water.

"Please," the voice said. "Everything here you have conjured up yourself. Drink. Eat. While your powers rejuvenate and grow."

"Who are you?" Mia called out.

"I am Feng, mother of djinn. Search your mind, you will find me."

"Where are you?" Mia turned circles, but so far, everything else in the room was dark.

"I am everywhere. I have always been here, waiting for you," Feng said. "Sit, drink, eat, rest."

Another light appeared over a soft-looking bed.

Had Mia really conjured everything herself? She had been thinking of a soft bed, food, water.

She stepped up to the table and frowned at all the colorful items.

"Pop-Tarts," she said, pointing to an empty spot on the table.

Suddenly, two blueberry Pop-Tarts appeared on a plate in the spot. She apparently was getting the hang of these new powers.

It appeared that all she had to do was want it badly enough and she made it happen.

Smiling, she sat down and poured herself a large glass of water and gulped the cold liquid down.

As she ate and drank, she searched her mind for any of her ancestors named Feng.

There, in the oldest memories given to her by her ancestors, was a young woman with jet-black hair and yellow eyes, dressed in a dress almost identical to the one she was now wearing. Feng was the mother of Fa Li, who was the first djinn to leave this place.

"You're the first," Mia said out loud to the empty room.

"I am," Feng answered.

"Why are you here?" She frowned, looking around.

"I never left Kòngbái," Feng answered.

"You never traveled to Earth?" Mia asked, feeling suddenly very tired.

"No, there was no need. Rest, my child, you will need it for what's to come," Feng said.

"What's to... what's coming?" Mia asked with a frown

as she glanced over towards the bed. It did look very inviting. How long had she traveled? How tired was she?

"The moment you arrived, they knew of your presence," Feng answered.

"They? Who?" Mia asked, suddenly on guard.

"The guardians. The ones who would bind you," Feng said. "Rest. By morning's light, your worlds will change. I can't help you in the physical realm, but I will never leave you while you're here," Feng added. "Rest."

Mia pulled off her sandals, crawled onto the bed, and drifted immediately off to sleep.

She woke to the sound of voices just outside the door. Just like the night before, the moment she wished for a cup of coffee, it appeared on the table in her favorite travel mug.

She needed to use a bathroom before she dealt with whatever awaited her outside, so she thought of one and another door appeared.

She took her coffee inside and freshened up as quickly as she could. She wished for clothes other than the long flowing dress but was disappointed when only a pair of sturdy boots and a leather belt appeared. The belt held a narrow sword made of what appeared to be solid gold. It had a jewel on it the same color as Feng's eyes.

At least she had a weapon. She tried to conjure up a gun or something more useful, but she was disappointed with the results of that as well.

She downed the rest of the coffee, set the mug down, and walked to the door. Her fingers tightened around the knob.

"I am with you," Feng said softly. "Always."

"Thanks," Mia answered, and opened the door to the voices.

Chapter Two

Lucas arrived in the place that Mia called the Void shortly after leaving Selene and Tara, his sisters, along with the rest of the odd gang at the large house in Hidden Creek, Georgia.

He'd been surprised he could travel there, since Mia claimed she was the only one who could travel to the realm. He wasn't sure how he'd done it, other than thinking really hard about her and his desire to help her.

He was tired, sore, and, for the first time in his life, bruised and battered. There were cuts and scratches all over his body, and he was pretty sure he had a black eye and a fat lip. All thanks to the battle they had fought and temporarily won against Moros, God of Doom. He was the reason that Lucas feared... well, everything.

His entire life, he'd seen visions of the god bringing about the destruction of the world. He'd spent most of his adult life shifting his world around to prevent the end, like game pieces in a battle.

Moros had used his son, Scott, as a vessel to sneak into the real world. But when Selene had confessed her love for

Scott, that had given her "ownership" of Scott, allowing them to beat Moros. At least temporarily.

Selene had confirmed that Moros was not able or allowed to possess what was no longer his. Selene and Scott loved one another, and the old magic of belonging to your loved ones won out in the end.

Looking around the Void, Lucas frowned at the vast flat land filled with caramel-colored sand. When he called out to Mia, he was shocked to hear a response.

"She is not here," a voice said on the wind.

"Where is she?" he asked.

"Over the mountains, you must travel, over the sea, you must sail, in order to find the djinn who holds the keys," the voice chanted, and then died out.

"I don't have time—" he started, but he gasped when two large iron shackles appeared on his wrists.

"You are bound to power," a new voice said much closer. "And power is to thee. Until she sets you free, you must come with me." A large creature with arms and legs the length of a football field appeared before him. It was hairless, eyeless, and mouthless. Its head was almost twenty stories above him. Its bulk blocked out the two suns that hung low in the sky.

Where in the hell had that thing appeared from? Why hadn't he seen it moments ago when he'd looked around?

It was then that he realized the shackles were attached to a chain held by the large creature.

"Let me go." He tried to pull against the chains with the superior strength that he'd had all of his life. When that didn't work, he tried to fly, something else he'd done for as long as he could remember. But he couldn't even jump high.

"Your power has no strength. You are as weak as a babe. I will take you to her. We shall see what we see." The being

The Void

started tugging on the chain, pulling Lucas along the sandy ground.

Suddenly, he realized that he had no powers in Mia's world. The only one with the power to save him now was Mia. The woman he'd come here to rescue.

How in the hell was he supposed to survive?

She'd made him and the others believe that there was nothing on this world. Hence the name.

Why call it the Void if there was something here?

He stumbled a few times trying to keep up with the large creature's pace. In the end, he was dragged most of the time.

Half of his time was spent in the air, swinging between the creature's gigantic legs as it walked. The other half, his feet dragged against the sand.

His arms and wrists hurt where the chains pulled him and he was desperate for food, water, sleep, and a piss.

When the giant leather-skinned creature stopped walking, they had reached the base of the mountains. Both the suns had finally sunk behind the peaks, cooling the evening off. He was slightly surprised to see three rather large moons rising in the sky. They were so close to one another that he wondered if they ever touched. But after getting a good look at them for a moment, he realized they were all on different orbits. The largest moon was far behind the smaller two and easily ten times the size of the first one.

"I cannot travel in rocks, you see. I am a creature of sand and sea," the creature said.

Lucas looked up as the chain started to slip from the beings' hands.

Finally, he was going to be able to break free.

He prepared himself to run, but just then another hand reached out from the tree line and easily caught the chain.

This creature was much smaller than the first but still as large as a house. It had skin made of the soft green moss usually found on forest floors or the sides of tree trunks. There were even small bird-like creatures flying around and landing on it.

Lucas couldn't see a face, much like with the other being, but something told him this creature had one.

"I will meet you on the mountain's other side. Until then, my sister will be your guide," the tan creature added.

Lucas watched the large creature that had been his captor disappear into the sand as if the entire floor opened up and swallowed it in one quick, silent swoosh. No wonder he hadn't seen it sneak up on him. It had most likely come up from the sand without him knowing.

"Come, mortal," the new voice said. "We have much ground to cover."

"I need rest," Lucas called out. "I need water, food, and rest." He yanked on the chains.

"Soon," the voice said back.

"You don't talk in riddles," he pointed out as they started walking. To Lucas's relief, this being walked more slowly and with much smaller steps. Thankfully, it appeared he wasn't going to be dragged during this portion of his trip.

"My brother likes theatrics," the creature answered.

"I'm Lucas," he said, trying to get some information as they went.

"Jain. My brother Proteus found you for Aynah. Word was sent for all creatures to be on alert for a mortal such as yourself," Jain answered.

They had moved beyond the first lower hills of the mountain and with each step she made further into the green forest, a brightly colored bloom appeared on her outer skin, as if the closer to the center of the mountains she got, the more she came alive. Or maybe the flowers came out because it was growing dark in the evening hours. Either way, he estimated they had less than an hour before it would be full dark.

"Aynah?" he asked.

"Yes, we have been asked to bring all outsiders directly to the city," Jain answered.

They walked for almost an hour, and he tried to gain as much knowledge from Jain as he could. Either the creature was cunning and knew how to keep her answers vague, or she really didn't know much beyond what she'd told him.

He had just repeated the same question for the third time when she stilled.

"I grow tired of your questions." She tugged on his chain and he fell face-first into the soft grass directly next to a small brook. "We rest here until light." Jain sat down next to him, shaking the ground when she did so. She rolled over and immediately fell asleep between two large trees.

When he realized that Jain still held tight to his chains, he put all thoughts of escape out of his mind.

Leaning forward, Lucas sipped from the cool clear water then relieved himself against the farthest tree that his chains would allow him to go to.

While he did so, he scanned his extensive knowledge of mythology for what he knew about an Aynah.

From what he could remember, an Aynah was a being that had six levels of incarnation, which he assumed meant she could take six different forms. Said to be the queen of all djinns. Could this be Mia?

Since this world was beyond the myths of Earth, he doubted the history he'd spent his entire life studying would be of much help.

He pulled out his phone and wasn't surprised to see there was no connection. But he snapped a few photos of Jain as she slept. Thankfully, he'd charged his phone before leaving and had some battery life left.

If they ever got out of this place, he'd enjoy showing his sisters the images.

As he settled into the soft mossy grass for the night, he scanned through the photos he'd taken over the past few weeks.

Looking down at the smiling faces of his two sisters, Selene and Tara, along with Scott and Colt, he realized just how happy the two couples were together. How well they fit together. Then he scrolled to a photo of him and Mia that Selene had taken at Mia's family's place just outside of Atlanta.

Mia's arm was thrown over Lucas's shoulder. Her tongue was out, shoved in the corner of her mouth as she stared at Lucas with a goofy look.

The image made him chuckle. Since the moment he'd met her, Mia had pulled out the humor Lucas had seemed to lack his entire life.

It wasn't as if he was always serious. Well, okay, he was. After all, he'd been around six years old when he'd found out that the fate of the world rested on his shoulders.

That was a heavy burden to bear. He'd spent his entire life, after that day, learning how to possibly stop its destruction. He'd studied every myth ever written in any history book in the hopes that it would help.

After all, he knew that the old gods were real, which meant that other myths might be true as well.

When he'd been old enough, he'd started to condition his body to aid in the fight that was to come. The day he'd learned of his other special skills, he hadn't been all that surprised.

The ability to fly, the extra strength, never being able to be hurt, those had just been an extra benefit. But the day he'd shifted into a large black wolf, that was the day everything had been made very clear to him.

That was the day he'd stopped being a kid. All laughter, all fun had fled from him. Until he'd met Selene and Mia.

Somehow, his sister and the djinn brought out something he'd buried deep inside himself long ago. Something that he hadn't known he'd been missing. Laughter.

He hadn't hesitated to volunteer to come and find and rescue Mia. Not after the feelings he'd felt for her since the moment he'd seen her.

He'd been slightly shocked at the zip of sexual tension he'd felt the moment he'd met her, something he'd never felt for anyone else. Ever.

Now, as he lay in the tall grass on a strange planet, probably billions and billions of light years from Earth, looking up at a very unfamiliar night sky with three moons, he wondered just what in the hell he was doing.

He hadn't questioned traveling to hell disguised as Cerberus, the three-headed hellhound that guards the gates of hell, to square off against the devil. But this, this just might be too much for him.

There was no use in trying to break free from the chains. They were obviously made of magic or some strange metal he'd never seen before.

He crossed his arms behind his head and lay there listening to Jain's deep breathing. Various night sounds filled the dark woods, none of which he feared.

Something told him that Jain and her brother Proteus were supposed to deliver him alive. Unharmed.

If this Aynah wasn't Mia, he wondered if she knew where Mia was. Was she safe? Did she still have her powers? If so, why hadn't she returned home?

As he drifted off to sleep, his dreams were filled with thoughts of Mia.

He woke when the chains were jerked and his arms twisted away and up until he was left hanging by his arms, looking directly into the eyes of Jain.

"You talk in your sleep," she said, narrowing her eyes. "What sort of being are you?"

"Human," he said, then he winced. "Well, sort of."

Her mossy eyebrows shot up. "Sort of?"

"I'm the son of gods. Raised by humans."

"What is... gods?" she asked, gently setting him back on the ground.

"Deities. Beings with great powers."

Jain laughed, causing the birds that nested in her mossy body to flutter away. "You have no powers. I would sense them."

He frowned. "It would appear that I don't here," he agreed.

"Aynah is the only one with power here," Jain said, tugging on the chain. "Come, my brother will be waiting."

He started to complain that he was hungry, but as they walked, Jain grabbed a couple of large blue fruits from the very tops of trees and handed him one.

"Eat." She tossed several in her mouth. Well, at least the spot he assumed was her mouth.

He could see now why he hadn't noticed her eyes before. They were hidden from below by the moss. From down here, he couldn't see them, which meant maybe she couldn't see him.

After eating the entire fruit, he tossed the large spiky

The Void

seed that had sat in the juicy middle of the fruit directly at her head.

At the last second, she tilted her head and the seed landed in what he thought of as her chin.

"Thank you," she said with a chuckle. "The hárpyia will enjoy using it in their nests."

He shrugged and continued walking. Obviously, she could see him.

"What kind of creature are you?" he asked, changing his tactics.

"We are nymphonids. My brothers, sisters, and me."

"Nymphs?" he asked, remembering the Greek myths about the creatures.

Jain glanced down at him. "Yes, you know of us?"

Lucas nodded. "I've heard of you. Never met one before yesterday."

Jain's body shifted slightly, and Lucas got the idea that she was smiling.

"We are pleased," she said, and then she continued walking.

"What happens when we reach the sea?" he asked.

"Proteus will carry you across the sea to the great city. We are not permitted to go beyond the walls. Only the Athaki can cross through the gates. Come, we have much land to travel."

They stopped by another brook when both suns were high above their heads. Jain produced a rather odd-looking gray fruit this time, which was somehow sour and salty at the same time. Still, he ate every bit of it as well as drank from the large river they had stopped to rest by.

It took them another two or three hours to reach the edge of the large body of water. He looked across the calm blue water and could see the tips of very tall shiny buildings on the other side. The light from the suns bounced off the glass of the skyscrapers. If he didn't know better, he'd believe it was any city in the States.

"That is the great city?" he asked Jain.

The creature glanced off across the sea then down at him and smiled. "Yes, that is Atlantis."

Chapter Three

Holy hell. What the actual...

Mia paced in an extremely plush room that reminded her of the fanciest hotel room that she'd ever seen in movies.

The walls were all covered with a marble-like material in soft white with gray streaks through it. There were hints of gold and silver, which lit up the entire room.

The ceilings were high and had multiple glass chandeliers hanging in various places.

In all, there were four rooms she had been locked in. There was a bedroom, which had a small sitting area next to a huge bed covered in soft teal comforters, and a beautiful bathroom, the walls of which were covered in some sort of granite in a busy pattern. There was a large circular shower in the middle of the room with glass walls. It was big enough for a dozen people to shower in. Off this room was a small closet filled with many different dresses, all of which fit her.

There was another bedroom across a large two-story living room space, which had three dark leather sofas all facing one another. The marble material covering those walls matched the ones in both bedrooms.

Wealth. The entire place screamed of money. At least it would if she was on Earth.

She was wringing her hands with worry, wishing more than anything for some way to communicate with the outside world.

She almost tripped on the thick rug that covered the light-colored wood on the floor, about the hundredth time doing so by her calculations. The loud voices were still echoing outside the building, many, many floors beneath her. Whether they were for or against her being there, she had no clue at this point.

Why in the hell hadn't her ancestors shown her this place? What was hidden in the Void?

Even Feng had gone MIA and had remained silent since her arrival in the city. Ever since her arrival, Mia had been stuck in this chamber, pacing. Worrying. Wondering. Her mind raced with so many questions.

Since her unceremonious arrival to the city, to a building somewhere among hundreds of other tall buildings in a city she had only seen for a few seconds from above, she'd been left alone.

The two women who had greeted her outside the door of the monolith hadn't said much to her. Instead, they had swooped her up and flown—yes, flown—her to the city. They had each held onto one of her arms without saying much. They hadn't even introduced themselves. They'd just swooped in, grabbed her, and hauled her away.

When they had landed on the roof where a dozen or more women stood, they had disappeared. The women had ushered her down a massive circular staircase.

She'd been stripped of all her possessions, which had

The Void

really only been her cell phone, and that didn't work anyway. Then she'd been shown into a large bathroom where a handful of women had removed her clothes and pulled her into a circular shower. She had stood under a powerful waterfall of water while they scrubbed her clean with long brushes.

From there, they had dried her off, tied her hair back in an intricate braid, and helped her into a light flowing gown in gold and teal colors in a material she'd never felt or seen before. It was so soft, it truly felt as if she was naked.

After she was dressed, strange-looking food had been delivered and she'd been left alone. At first, she'd avoided eating it. She'd even conjured up some food herself. But then she'd grown curious and had sampled several different items. It was all delicious. Extremely so.

The soft comfortable bed had called to her, and she'd removed the dress and pulled on the soft teal bed gown that had been left for her.

The following morning, she changed into another teal dress that had been left for her. She'd tried the door, but it had been locked, so she'd started pacing. Food was delivered. Empty trays were removed. New clothes were brought in.

No one talked to her. When she asked questions, they just bowed their heads and nodded like they didn't understand her.

On the evening of the second day, a group of women came into her rooms again. Once more she was showered, her hair done up in another fancy braid piled on top of her head.

She was helped into another gown, this one a darker shade of teal. Rings and jewelry were placed on her fingers, wrist, ears, and around her neck.

Once she had been dressed and prepared, she was guided down many hallways and up so many stairs that she felt breathless when they finally reached the top. She walked through two carved wood doors and stepped out into the large outdoor chamber that she had first arrived at. This time the space was filled with hundreds of people, who were dressed much like she was, with the exception of the heavy jeweled crown that had been placed on her head.

When she entered, everyone fell silent. Every eye watched her as she moved to the front of the room.

None of the spaces here were like she'd imagined they would be. While it was obvious that the buildings were old —older than anything on Earth—everything looked modern.

She didn't notice any of the classic building styles found on Earth—Renaissance, Gothic, Greek, or even Victorian eras.

The space they were in now was an outdoor roof garden that looked out over a huge modern-looking city. She could see tall buildings in the distance, all of them much lower than the one they were on now.

Black shiny tile floors gleamed on the pathway, and cream and teal carpets guided her across the space.

Trees of every color surrounded the crowd. Plants of different shapes and sizes sat on either side of the doorway and front area.

The furniture in the rooms she had stayed in had been pretty standard, with the exception of some of the color choices. Gold and teal were the preferred shades in most of the rooms she'd been in.

Now, as she stood under the three moons, she glanced up and noticed the intricate glass chandeliers that hung from large beams that crossed high overhead.

Every eye was on her. She turned and saw a large

golden chair on a large pedestal in front of everyone else. Both of the suns were setting directly behind the large golden throne.

The two women who had kidnapped her and flown her here were standing at the top of the dozen or more stairs to the throne area at the end of the aisle. Lifting her chin, Mia slowly made her way towards them.

In her mind, she likened the scene to a wedding. While she wasn't in all white and the man of her dreams wasn't waiting for her at the altar, she felt as if whatever happened now was going to be life altering.

Both of the women appeared to be in their mid-twenties. One was dressed in a long flowing silver and lavender gown, much like Mia was. The closer Mia got, the more she realized that this woman's dark skin practically glowed, as if it had been sprayed with tiny golden sparkles. A large sleek silver crown sat on top of her jet-black hair.

The other woman was dressed in a flowing golden gown. Her paler skin appeared as if it were made of stardust, and her long golden hair held a crown much like Mia and the other woman were wearing, but this one was gold and it gleamed so brightly it hurt Mia's eyes.

When they'd kidnapped her, she had thought that both of them had been pretty, but now she could see that they were absolutely gorgeous. They could have easily been supermodels. Instantly, Mia felt short and boring.

The woman dressed in lavender moved forward slightly and lifted her arms. Everyone gathered fell silent once more.

"Welcome, Mia Li, daughter of Malik al-Ahmar," the woman said clearly. "We are sorry for keeping you waiting so long for answers. We needed to be assured of a few things and had to get everything in order for our departure."

"We have been expecting you for a very long time," the other woman added.

Since her arrival, this was the first time she'd heard someone speak English. Or for that matter, speak to her at all.

Then Mia frowned. Her father's name wasn't Malik al-Ahmar. It was Ken. Ken Li. Maybe they had the wrong person?

Both women looked down at her, waiting.

"Thank you," she said, unsure of what to say. Should she point out that they had made a mistake? They had obviously kidnapped the wrong person.

"I am Elpis, this is my sister Pandora." The woman turned to the other woman in gold. Sister? The two women were polar opposites and looked nothing alike.

Then she ran over the names in her mind.

Elpis. Pandora.

That couldn't be right. Could it?

Had she just gotten very lucky? Standing in front of her were the two people they had been told by the fates that they would need if they were going to win their battle with Moros.

Mia knew that, according to legend, Elpis was hope. Hope that had been locked away in Pandora's box. Elpis was technically Moros's sister, the only entity that could actually bind him. Which is why he'd tricked Pandora into locking her away.

"Please." Pandora motioned towards the throne. "It's past time you took your rightful place."

"Me?" Her voice squeaked and then, to her horror, echoed in the massive space so that she heard herself several times.

Elpis smiled. "Yes, you, djinn. You are the daughter of

The Void

Malik al-Ahmar and Feng Li. The first of their kind. The creators of this realm."

"You are the rightful ruler of Atlantis," Pandora added with a wave of her hands.

The burst of laughter that exploded from Mia's chest echoed into the evening air.

"Seriously?" She glanced around. "Atlantis? This is Atlantis? The legendary city that disappeared eons ago?"

Elpis smiled and then nodded. "These are your people. The Athaki." She motioned around them. "It is time my sister and I take our leave." Elpis started to move aside, then she stopped and motioned towards the throne and waited until Mia climbed the stairs.

"I really think you have the wrong person," Mia said softly as she stopped next to them.

Both Elpis and Pandora smiled back at her.

"We have been waiting for you for thousands of millennia," Elpis said, touching her arm lightly.

Mia frowned. "You don't look a day over a hundred millennia," she said dryly.

Was this all a joke?

Both Elpis and Pandora smiled back at her as if they didn't get the joke.

"We are endless," Pandora said softly.

"It's time my sister and I took our rightful places in the universe and prepared for what is to come. It's you who must lead your people through what is to take place here next," she said with a slight frown. "You and the other with power who has followed you here are needed for the battle between light and dark before you can return to your new home. A warning..." She paused, her eyes searching Mia's. "The war of light against dark can only be won if you are together in all things."

"Who?" Mia asked with a frown. "Who is the other?"

"His powers are held back for now. Only you have the power to set them free," Pandora said without answering Mia's question. "Even now, he travels across the desert, mountains, and waters to rescue you."

"He cannot take his animal form, nor does he have his powers of flight and strength," Elpis added. "Which will all be needed if you are to survive, together."

"Lucas?" Mia gasped. "He's here? In the Void?" She glanced towards the sky, hoping to see him flying towards her. Then Elpis's words sunk in. He didn't have his powers. He couldn't fly.

Mia turned back towards the women, a little more anxious now that she knew Lucas was on his way to her.

"We will meet again soon. You will know us, we won't know you." Elpis leaned closer. "The next time we meet, it will be your task to guide us," she added with a wink.

"What?" Mia frowned, shaking her head slightly.

"Soon you will understand everything," Pandora said.

Both women turned their eyes towards the sky just as the two suns slipped behind the horizon and the last rays of daylight disappeared.

As she watched, they lifted up into the sky and disappeared into nothingness directly in front of everyone, leaving a trail of sprinkling gold and silver stardust in their wake.

Mia would have thought that the crowd would be as shocked to see two women disappear into thin air as she was, but no one seemed surprised at all. Instead, they looked at her in wonder and in question.

Now, standing in front of a throne, her throne, she looked out at the faces staring back at her and wondered

The Void

what they wanted. They were waiting. On her. To do what? Make a speech?

What should she say? What could she say? Did they even understand her?

Her entire life she'd believed this place was void of life. A dead realm. She'd never thought to travel anywhere other than the cave and the desert she always appeared in. She'd never once thought to explore it.

Clearing her throat, she straightened.

"Hi," she said with a smile. The room remained silent. "Thank you, everyone, for the warm welcome I've been given. It looks like I'll be your genie for the time being." She waited a heartbeat. "I... didn't even know this place existed. I mean, I'd heard rumors, legends really." She shook her head and cleared her thoughts. "I mean, everyone has heard of Atlantis. It's... everything I thought it would be." She bit her lip to force herself to stop talking. "Except the flying cars." She winced and held in a groan. She really should shut up. Turning to the nearest person, she asked, "I don't suppose anyone could fill me in on how things work around here?"

Suddenly, a middle-aged woman appeared by her side. The woman was practically frowning at her.

"I have been chosen to be your advisor," the woman said with a slight curtsy. "I am Beth," the woman added. There was a thick accent but Mia couldn't place its origins. Probably because she was on a different freaking planet. She mentally kicked herself for being stupid.

It was then that it hit Mia. Everyone in the room—no, scratch that, everyone in the realm—expected her to rule, to lead them through a war. What had Elpis called it? The war of light against dark.

Suddenly, she felt light-headed. If they hadn't been

standing outside in the cool night breeze, she would have excused herself to grab some air. Instead, she sat down on the throne behind her and took several long, deep breaths until she felt under control again.

"What exactly do you know about Atlantis?" Beth asked moving closer to her.

Mia gripped the arms of the chair until her knuckles turned white. "Nothing," she admitted. "Nothing that is true, at any rate."

"Well, there's only one place to start, I suppose. At the beginning…" Beth started, but Mia was too focused on the crowd of people still watching her.

What did they want? Why were they still standing there? What were they waiting for?

During this time, Beth hovered beside her, chatting non-stop about… well, Mia didn't know. She wasn't paying attention.

"Which you will meet after your companion gets here. He will call for you when he is ready," Beth finished.

"I…" She frowned. "Did they"—she motioned to the air where the two women had just vanished—"say something about Lucas being brought here?"

"As we speak, your companion is crossing the mountains. He should be here by tomorrow's supper," Beth answered.

At that moment, Mia's stomach let out a loud growling noise.

Beth's eyebrows shot up at the noise.

"I don't suppose tonight's supper is soon?" Mia asked.

"It is already waiting for you in the grand hall," Beth answered, then she stood back, waiting for Mia.

"Why are they all still here?" she whispered.

The Void

Beth leaned a little closer and lowered her voice. "They are waiting for you to dismiss them."

Mia puffed out a breath of air. "Right." She stood up and with a big smile on her face, loudly said, "Thank you all for coming today. You are dismissed."

No one moved.

Mia leaned towards Beth and asked. "Why didn't that work?"

Beth shook her head. "We are all hoping to see a bit of your magic. The guardians have told us great details about you. We are excited to see what you can do, how you will save us from the darkness."

Guardians? She must mean Elpis and Pandora.

Mia swallowed the lump in her throat. She wanted to tell the woman and the room that she didn't do magic tricks, but she tried to think of something she could do to appease the crowd.

Then she smiled. Since meeting Selene and seeing her neat trick of creating flames with a snap of her fingers, she'd practiced her own trick much like it.

Lifting her hands and pulling the sleeves of her long dress back, she held her hands high up and willed what was deep inside her to build.

At first, it was just a few sparks that leapt from her palms. Then, a large ball of fire as hot as the sun floated slowly into the sky. It rose almost a hundred feet up before bursting into tiny pieces that gently rained down over the crowd, who immediately burst into cheers. Then, as if on cue, each of them bowed as low as they could and started to chant her name.

This time, when she raised her hands, the entire room quieted.

"Thank you, now please, return to your homes, enjoy your dinners." To her delight, the space emptied quickly.

"Is that how you plan to save us?" Beth asked as she led Mia inside and down a larger circular staircase. She hadn't been brought up to the roof this way and was totally lost in the massive building. She couldn't even remember what floor her rooms had been on before.

There was no writing or signs to guide the way around the enormous structure.

"I..." Mia frowned. "No, sorry, that's just a parlor trick. I'm surprised it worked this time. I've only done that twice now." She shrugged.

Beth stopped outside two wooden doors that were two stories high.

"I suppose you have time to hone your skills. After your companion arrives." Beth stood back as two men in what could be described as military uniforms opened the doors for them.

There, in the largest room she'd ever seen, was everyone who had been upstairs. They all sat at tables, waiting for her. When she entered, every single head turned her way.

Once more, they waited and watched, wanting something from her.

Mia's shoulders slumped for a split second. She'd hoped for a moment alone. A quiet dinner to reflect. Instead, she sat at the head table under everyone's watchful eye as she ate alone.

Chapter Four

By the time Proteus arrived at the water's edge, the suns were high overhead. Lucas and Jain had waited, talking and snacking on fresh fruit that grew by the edge of the vast sea.

He'd enjoyed his time with her, oddly enough. But he wasn't looking forward to being pulled around by Proteus again. He still had no idea how the large creature was going to carry him across the dark waters.

When Proteus finally arrived, Lucas understood how. The being was towing a large boat at the end of a thick chain.

Lucas wondered if the creature was actually swimming in the murky water or simply walking along the bottom of it. Proteus didn't appear to be working that hard, yet he and the boat were traveling at high speed.

"We part in the flesh," Jain said as the boat bumped ashore at Lucas's feet. Then she turned back towards the trees and called over her shoulder as she left, "Until I am needed again."

"Thank you," he called after her as she disappeared.

Less than two steps inside the thick green brush, he could no longer make out her form.

"Across the sea we travel now," Proteus started as Lucas climbed aboard the boat. "Sailing under the twin suns' warm glow," Proteus continued as they started to glide quickly across the sea. Lucas held onto the side railing since the boat was traveling very fast. "To save this realm from the darkness that comes, so that heroes may unite and beat the drums. With courage and strength, they face their fears, braving the night, wiping away tears." Proteus's words grew into a song as the massive creature pulled him across the water. He sang, "Through battles fought, and trials endured, their spirits untamed, their hearts assured. Together they stand, in unity strong, defending the realm, righting every wrong. In darkness they shine, a beacon of light, guiding the way through the endless night. For in their resolve, hope will ignite, to save this realm, they'll forever fight."

Lucas wondered vaguely what the song was about. The closer they got to the city, the larger it appeared.

Jain had filled him in on a few things about Atlantis. The people that lived there were called the Athaki, not the Atlanteans.

They were ruled by Aynah, their queen or god. The way Jain talked about it, he leaned more towards god.

For thousands of millennia, the twin guardians had protected the realm, until one day when Aynah would return to win some great war that had been foretold eons ago.

Having grown up believing in fairytales, Lucas had no doubt that everything Jain told him was true.

He didn't know where Mia fit into the story, nor did he yet know why he no longer had his powers. What mattered

The Void

was rescuing Mia and returning to Earth as quickly as possible.

They still had so much to do to prepare for their next battle there.

By his estimate, it took almost an hour to cross the water. When he glanced back at the path he'd traveled, he was in awe of the beauty of the forest and mountains behind him. When he had walked towards the mountains in the desert, they'd appeared to be lower, almost hills. From this vantage point, he could see the highest peak. Cliffs butted up against almost a quarter of the water, while the low rolling hills where he'd come from surrounded the rest. The mountain peaks sat beyond all of it, as if shadowing the sea and growing from its depths.

He had half expected Proteus to deliver him to a dock or port of some sorts. Instead, there was a band of red sand almost a mile wide that sat around the entire city, separating it from the water.

"To the Aynah, go directly. The Kri's visions may cause thee, Hinder not thy path, resolutely. Embrace the journey, ardently." Proteus pointed a very long finger out of the water towards the city. Then he lifted his fingers towards him, and the chains on Lucas's wrists disappeared.

"Got it." Lucas rubbed his wrists and glanced out over the mile or so of sand he still had to pass through. "Don't dawdle," he said and then turned back. "You're not coming with me?" he asked Proteus.

The creature shook once, then completely disappeared into the dark water with nothing more than a little splash.

"I'll take that as a no," he said to himself. After glancing around, he jumped off the boat and landed softly on the red sand.

For the next few minutes, he walked, his eyes on the

city as thoughts of Mia flooded his mind. Was she okay? Had she taken the same path he had? Had she been kidnapped by the same two creatures and brought here?

How had he come to care so much for the little genie? They'd only known one another for a few weeks. Or had it been months? Time was a tricky thing when traveling between realms.

Still, the thought of being able to see her again caused a little spike of interest and something else in him. The truth was, she excited him. He'd looked forward to her quick and witty banter every day.

She was the only woman he'd known that hadn't treated him like she wanted him because of his position and wealth. He'd been adopted by a wealthy couple and when he'd been old enough and ready, he'd taken over his father's powerful company. That had some perks and some downfalls.

Women were easily had. Most sought him out and were willing to overlook his... quirks. But he had never gotten close to anyone. The longest relationship he'd had was a weekend tryst. But they had gotten what they wanted from him and vice versa, so there hadn't been any issues.

Mia was the only woman he'd thought of being with, yet he had held back for some reason.

Why was that? He'd desperately wanted to explore that, but there had been a world to save. He'd told himself that if they were successful in fighting off Moros, and they both made it out alive, he'd get to the root of his feelings for her.

He almost tripped in the deep sand and focused on the city ahead of him.

Jain had mentioned that only the Athakis were allowed in the city. Why?

With each step he took, he had more questions.

How was he going to find Mia in such a large city? Why

were his powers still gone? Would they ever come back? When he almost tripped in the sand again, he had a new question. Why hadn't they build the city closer to the water?

Suddenly, he stopped and frowned at the vision in front of him. He must have been walking for more than an hour, yet the city didn't appear to be any closer.

Turning around, he gasped at the sight of the water only a couple of feet behind him.

That couldn't be right. He took a giant step towards the city and turned back towards the water. Again, it was as if he hadn't even moved.

He looked down at the sand and at his footprints.

There were two deep impressions from when his feet had hit the shore from the boat, then one step forward and nothing. His feet were there. He was standing only one step into the band of red sand.

Yet, his body ached from the hour or so of walking across the space. He was thirsty and a little sunburnt from the heat of the suns bouncing off the bright red granules.

After his fourth attempt to move forward, he stilled and remembered Proteus's words. "Hinder not thy path, resolutely."

This must be the Kri Proteus was talking about. Was it the red sand or some sort of invisible being keeping him from getting closer to the city?

Taking a deep breath, he focused solely on getting to Mia. Only Mia. With each step, he focused on being one step closer to her.

The suns beat down on him and there were times he had to force his mind not to waver. Mia. Only Mia. Closer to her. One step closer.

When he noticed that he was indeed moving closer to

the city, he wanted to rejoice. Instead, he chanted. Mia. Closer to Mia. One step closer to Mia.

He lost track of time. Lost track of how many steps he had taken. How thirsty he was. How tired. How hot.

Only Mia mattered now. Getting to her.

When he finally felt some shade envelop him, he glanced up and noticed that the two suns were a lot lower in the sky. It wouldn't be long now before it was dark.

Returning his gaze to the city, he gasped and almost fell backward. Directly in front of him, less than an arm's reach away, was a huge iron door. There were odd-looking symbols on it—a long slash in the middle with two triangles turned onto their sides.

He glanced up at the tall wall. Somehow, he'd reached the city without even knowing it.

When he took a step forward to knock on the doors, they slid open smoothly and silently before he could touch them.

The suns were directly in front of him, and he blinked at their light and then saw that Mia stood on the other side of the doorway in an old-fashioned gown. Her long hair flowed around her shoulders, swaying in the cool breeze.

"You came," Mia said with a smile.

"I came here to rescue you," he answered.

"I don't need rescuing." She smiled at him.

"I gather that." He frowned as he glanced around the empty city. "So, this is Atlantis?"

Instead of answering, she took his hand and pulled him further into the city.

"Isn't it simply amazing?" she said, practically dancing as they walked through the clean, wide city streets. "Let's stay here forever."

The Void

There was no clutter, trash, cars, or people that he could see. But he was tired, hungry, in desperate need of water.

Mia stopped suddenly and turned towards him. "Thirsty? Hungry? You're probably starving after your journey."

"You've no idea," he said dryly.

Mia motioned with her hand and suddenly a table with two chairs appeared directly in front of them, a tray of food sitting on it.

She moved forward, poured some clear liquid into a tall glass, and held it out for him.

Then she waited and watched as he lifted the glass to his lips.

He couldn't explain it, but immediately he felt as if something was off.

Mia was being... different. Gone was the quick banter, the little jabs she'd take at him with humor. This Mia was too accepting. Too accommodating. Much like all the other women he'd been with up to this point in his life.

Something was definitely off.

Instead of drinking the liquid, he set the glass down on the table.

Mia's brows furrowed slightly.

"Why don't you show me around first?" he asked.

Mia frowned and took up the glass. "First, drink." She held the glass out towards him. "So we can be together forever."

"No, thank you." He tilted his head and ran his eyes over her.

Why hadn't he seen it before? Not only was she acting strange, but Mia's face was off. Her eyes were too far apart and a completely different shade of brown.

He'd been so happy to see her, so happy to be out of the desert, that he hadn't paid attention.

"Drink," she screeched in a deep voice as she shoved the glass towards him.

"I don't think so." He crossed his arms over his chest, then closed his eyes and said in a firm voice, "Mia. Only Mia. Closer to her. One step closer." He took a giant step in his mind. Then another as he continued to chant.

The creature that had been portraying Mia screamed with each step he took.

Even the thirst and hunger he'd been feeling disappeared the farther he went. As he moved, he kept his eyes closed, chanting louder and louder.

When he came up against a wall, instead of opening his eyes, he felt around. It took him a long time to find a door handle, or what he thought of as a door handle. It was a large circle attached to a plank of wood.

When he pulled on it, the door silently opened.

It wasn't until he was inside that he finally opened his eyes. He had to blink a few times.

When he finally focused, he realized that Mia stood just inside of the doorway.

This version of her was dressed in a long flowing gown and her hair was braided in two braids that looped over her head and twisted around into a bun piled on her head.

She looked... amazing.

Was this a vision or trick as well? If so, this time, he didn't care. He was too tired and needed the reprieve.

He ran his eyes over her and relaxed.

Why had he questioned how he felt about her? It was so obvious now. He'd fight through hell, the Void, and the Kri, if that's what the red sand had been, to get to her.

The Void

She was unlike anyone he'd ever had feelings for or even known before.

She stood a few yards away from him, smiling at him as if he'd just run a bloody marathon. A roar of cheers erupted and he realized that she wasn't alone. There were crowds of people gathered around her. The women were dressed in long gowns like she was. The men wore pants and odd-looking shirts with long sleeves and big buttons. The scene was almost like some sort of celebration parade.

He moved towards her, still wondering if this was another vision. The streets appeared a lot like they had in the earlier vision, clean and clutter free. There appeared to be no cars, and the streets were a lot narrower than most city streets he was used to. The tall glass buildings hovered overhead, filling the skies with their gleaming glass exteriors.

He stopped in front of Mia and swayed, and she rushed the last few steps and wrapped her arms around him.

"You came for me," she said into his chest. "I'm so happy you're here."

She felt so soft. So... inviting. So real.

"Is this real?" he asked with a frown, unsure of anything at this point.

Without hesitating, Mia reached up and pinched his arm. Hard.

"Ouch." He chuckled. "Okay, so you're real. This time."

"This time?" She frowned up at him.

"Long story." He glanced around with a sigh. "Any chance there's some food nearby?"

"Supper is waiting for us." She motioned with her head. "Back at... well, I don't know what they call the building I've been staying at. There aren't any signs." She shrugged.

"Not even street signs. I have no clue how they know how to get around."

"I live in New York, and I thought that city was big. This place..." He shook his head as he looked around as they started walking. "At least from what I could tell on my long trip here, it is easily ten times the size of Manhattan."

Mia leaned towards him and lowered her voice. "It's deceiving," she whispered. "From what I can tell, that's everyone who lives here." She motioned with her head behind them.

He glanced back at the hundred or so people that followed and watched them.

"What?" He turned to Mia, who nodded her head. "Food first." She took his arm in hers and continued walking. "We can talk when we're alone," she added under her breath.

He nodded in agreement. Besides, he was starving and very thirsty.

They made their way through the narrow streets, winding around until they were surrounded by tall buildings. Then they stepped into a massive building that took up at least two city blocks, where a middle-aged woman stood just inside the doors waiting for them.

"Beth, this is Lucas. Lucas, Beth is my advisor." She waved her hand towards the woman.

He nodded and the woman curtsied in his direction and then motioned for them to follow her.

They climbed a wide circular staircase and stepped into a large dining hall.

"We're to sit at the head table," Mia said.

As they made their way across the room, the entire crowd that had followed them filled the space as well.

"Everyone eats dinner together," Mia added softly. "At least, that's what I can tell."

He sat next to Mia, and they both waited until every last person was sitting.

"Everything here is delicious," Mia said as large platters of various foods were set in front of them. "Water." She held up a metal canister in his direction. "Drink."

He hesitated a second until he watched her lift her own container and drink. Then he drank the entire thing in one swallow.

Chapter Five

Mia could see that Lucas was jumpy. She didn't know why but figured once they were alone in her rooms, they could talk.

In the past day, she'd done all she could to learn everything about Atlantis.

First off, there were no children here. Not a single one. The youngest person that she'd seen so far was the young girl that filled their drinks. By her estimate the girl was around fifteen or sixteen at the most.

Second, the two hundred or so people that filled the dining room now were the only ones that lived in the massive city. Every single one lived in the building they were in now. Each floor was separated into living quarters, determined by a person's duties. Her rooms filled an entire floor and were near the throne room in the rooftop garden, which everyone had access to.

Third, when everyone had been calling Lucas her companion, what they really meant was her betrothed or husband. They expected to crown Lucas as some sort of king in a ceremony soon.

Which made being around him very awkward. Just knowing that she had to explain it to him put her on edge.

Lastly, no one in the city ever left it. Not one person had exited the city walls since the beginning of time. Nor had any other creatures or beings come into the city. She and Lucas were the first since the guardians had appeared to protect them.

Mia got the impression that no one cared to leave the city, not that they were afraid to.

"More water?" Mia asked him when he was done drinking the entire container. When he nodded, she waved her container, and the young girl rushed over to refill both of their drinks. She had yet to ask her what her name was. So far, she had only learned Beth's name.

When more food trays were delivered, they ate together in silence. Lucas appeared as if he'd been starving. She ate as much as she could, knowing full well that there were only two meals a day instead of the standard three, breakfast and supper. Breakfast was served just after sunrise and supper served just after sunset.

When they were done eating, she leaned closer to Lucas. "They're expecting you to say something." She nudged him and he glanced around.

"Me?" He frowned, seeing that the attention of everyone in the room was on him.

She nodded in response. "I was told by Beth that its customary. She claims that no one has ever been able to get through the Kri." She waited for a beat. "But I have no clue what that is."

"A desert that makes you hallucinate," he answered under his breath.

"Really?" She frowned at him. When he nodded, she continued. "Well, it's customary to share your experience."

The Void

He frowned. "I'd rather not."

She touched his arm. "Just... say something. We don't want to be rude."

He nodded in agreement.

When she stood, everyone in the room grew quiet and stopped eating.

"Tonight, we celebrate the first Kri crossing," she said, repeating the words Beth had given her earlier. "My companion, Lucas Romano." Mia felt her face heat slightly at her acknowledgement of their relationship in the Athakis' eyes. She sat down when Lucas stood.

"Thank you, everyone, for such a warm welcome." Everyone cheered for a few seconds. When the crowd grew quiet, he continued. "Over the past few days as I crossed the land, I noticed the beauty of it. It's natural wonder..."

Mia noticed instantly that the crowd was frowning and apparently so did Lucas, because he changed tactics quickly.

"I'm thankful that I've finally made it to such a wonderful place." He motioned around them. "And have been welcomed with such fervor. The crossing was difficult at times." He glanced down at her and she noticed something deep in his eyes. "I'm thankful I've finally made it here." He nodded once before sitting down as everyone cheered.

"Do you have someplace we can talk, privately?" he asked quietly, leaning closer.

Mia nodded and then stood. "Please, enjoy the rest of your meal and have a wonderful evening," she said to everyone in the room. When everyone continued to watch her, she sighed and once more raised her hands and shot a ball of fire into the high ceilings of the room.

She and Lucas exited as everyone cheered and celebrated her little trick.

"Please," Mia said, holding up her hands. "Lucas and I wish to retire now," she told Beth, who had started to follow them up the stairs. "I believe I can find my way back to my rooms."

Beth nodded and then returned to the dining hall.

"What—" Lucas started to say as they climbed the stairs.

Mia reached out and took his hand, shushing him. Then she motioned to the guards stationed on each floor that they passed by.

When they had climbed a dozen or so flights of stairs, she made her way down the hallway to the double doors that opened up into her rooms, the same rooms she'd been in those first nights and had returned to last night after her official crowning ceremony. Or whatever they called it when she was given full power of this realm.

Once she shut the door behind them, she sighed and leaned back against the closed doors, tossing her crown onto a table that sat just inside the doors.

"Why didn't you return home?" Lucas asked first.

"I can't." She threw up her hands. "I've tried." She closed her eyes and willed herself back home. She opened them again with a groan. "See."

"Okay," he said slowly with a frown. "Did you just try going without me?"

She shrugged again. "You don't have your powers either." She motioned to him.

"No, I don't. But you still have your powers." He waved his hand towards the door. "That grand finale was new."

"Yes, I've been working on that trick ever since I saw Selene do it." She smiled and slipped off her heeled shoes,

The Void

then reached up and untied her hair, letting it fall over her shoulders. "I've also got a few new tricks up my sleeves since arriving."

Lucas remained quiet, standing just inside the door as she made herself more comfortable.

"What?" She frowned at him when he didn't say anything.

"Are you sure you're real?" he surprised her by asking.

She frowned and moved closer to him. "Just what did happen to you in the Kri?" she asked.

He took a deep breath and closed his eyes for a moment.

"Kri's visions may cause thee, Hinder not thy path, resolutely, embrace the journey, ardently," he said in a strange voice. At first, she'd believed he was in a trance, but then he opened his eyes and smiled at her. "I saw... things."

"Okay," she said slowly, her eyes running over him. "You look tired, and in need of a shower."

He glanced down at his dirty clothes and groaned. "I don't suppose they have indoor plumbing?"

She smiled. "They do, the bathroom is in there." She stopped him from leaving by holding up her hand. "Here, I'll conjure you some clean clothes."

"You can do that?" he asked.

She shrugged. "Since I've been here, I've discovered that I can do a lot of new things." She held up her hand and smiled when a large chocolate ice cream cone with sprinkles appeared in her hands. Taking a bite, she waved towards the bed, and a pair of jeans and a black T-shirt in his size appeared. They were folded nicely on the edge of the bed. She'd seen him wear the same outfit a few times before and liked the way he looked in it.

"Impressive," he said as he bent and picked up the items before disappearing into the bathroom.

While he showered, she thought of how nice it was not to have to hide her abilities from him or, at this point, anyone else.

Never in her life had she been able to do that with anyone outside of her family. It had been so hard to keep who she was, what she was, from everyone she met. If someone was in trouble, she'd have to weigh the cost of being caught if she helped them. Her entire life, she'd been raised to help the less fortunate. But being caught was not an option.

Glancing at herself in the mirror, she thought quickly about changing out of the dress. Even though it was comfortable, it was a little formal for sitting around and having a chat with Lucas.

But what should she wear?

She stared at her reflection while she finished off the ice cream treat.

She'd always believed herself to be dull looking. Sure, her long hair was shiny and rich black color. There were a few honey-colored highlights that she'd added a while back. Plus, when she did try to curl it, thankfully, the curls stayed in place with the help of some product. The way the women had braided it and pulled it up was kind of new and far more exciting than the ponytail she always wore.

She was slender and only five-three, the tallest in her family. Yet most everyone here was shorter than her, even the men.

Lucas was well over six foot and practically towered over everyone here.

What she wanted to change into were some soft yoga pants and a large comfortable T-shirt. Instead, she conjured up something a little more... Atlantean.

The sundress was extremely comfortable and a little

sexy. She hardly wore dresses at home. Not that she didn't like to, but her job at the coffee shop didn't exactly require she wear them. Nor did her personal life. Hell, the last time she'd dated anyone had been in high school. Being a djinn really did cut into your personal life. She knew for a fact that the last six djinn in the Li family had all died lonely and unwed.

She had been determined after hitting her teens to break that pattern. Then she'd gone on her first date and realized how hard her powers made it for her to fit into real life.

Not only had it been impossible to hide what she was, but after a while she'd grown bitter about how she'd been treated and judged by others at the slightest hint that she was special. Until she'd met Selene and Scott, and then Lucas. She glanced towards the bathroom door and smiled. Damn. She was thankful he was the one who had come to rescue her.

She wondered just how he planned on doing that. Frowning, she sat on the edge of the bed.

He had no powers. She was supposed to give his powers back to him, but she didn't know how to do that either.

Elpis and Pandora hadn't mentioned how she was to achieve that task. Nor had they offered up any real advice as to what was to come after.

When Lucas walked out of the bathroom, dressed in the clothes she'd provided for him, she was deep in thought. So many questions ran through her mind that she had a slight headache.

"Just how, exactly, were you planning on rescuing me?" she asked him.

He frowned and then sat down in a chair opposite the bed.

His dark hair was still wet from the shower and several days' worth of stubble was still on his face. She really liked it and was thankful she'd forgotten to conjure up something so that he could shave. It made him look more... dangerous.

"I haven't figured that out yet. I had expected to have my abilities still." He looked down at his hands.

"They told me that I'm supposed to give them back to you," she said, and he frowned at her.

"Who told you?" he asked. "And how are you supposed to do that?"

"I don't know, but I can try." She poured everything she had into the task.

When Lucas frowned and shook his head, she relaxed.

"Elpis and Pandora are the ones who told me that I'd be able to return your powers," she said.

"They were here?" he asked, sitting up a little, sounding excited.

"They're gone. They disappeared last night. I gather that they were the guardians of this place until I was made official last night when I was given that." Mia motioned to the crown.

"Elpis is the essence of hope and Moros's sister. Pandora is supposed to unleash Elpis so she can fight her brother," he said in a tone that told her he was replaying the information.

Mia nodded. "They claimed to be sisters."

Lucas was quiet for a moment, as if he was taking it all in, trying to figure things out, much like she had the night before. He leaned back and looked relaxed and very tired. "So you're what around here, queen?"

She shrugged. "I suppose. They don't treat me like one, though. More like a..." She frowned as she thought about it.

The Void

"Hero or protector. They follow me around like I'm a freaking rock star."

"I noticed that. Does anyone else have abilities here?"

She shook her head. "There aren't any children either. When I asked, it was as if no one knew what I was talking about."

"Strange." He shifted slightly.

"They never leave the city. No one has ever. Nor has anyone besides us ever been able to pass in."

"How did you get here? If you didn't cross the Kri?" he asked.

"Elpis and Pandora flew me here," she said with a shrug.

"But they didn't tell you how to give me back my abilities?"

She shook her head and leaned back on the bed. "Nope."

"Okay." He glanced around. "As much as I want to continue this conversation, it was a very long trip across the red sand."

"Red sand?" She frowned. "What red sand?"

"Outside the city walls," he answered. "The Kri."

"There's no red sand outside the walls. The city is surrounded by water." She motioned towards the windows, but it was dark outside, so they wouldn't be able to see anything.

Instead of responding to that, Lucas ran his eyes over her. "You look happy," he said a while later.

She thought about it. "I suppose I am. I can't explain it, but I never felt like I fit in on Earth. I was a nobody. An outcast."

Lucas surprised her by moving to sit next to her on the bed and taking her hand in his.

"You are exactly the opposite of a nobody," he said

softly, then he shocked her by leaning closer and placing his lips over hers. "Yup, real," he said before taking the kiss deeper.

At the very moment his lips touched hers, energy built up in her very core. She'd experienced a few moments of intense power in her life. The day she'd gotten her powers, and the day she'd first shifted into her dog form.

This, however, was something altogether different.

Chapter Six

What in the hell was that? Lucas didn't know what had caused him to kiss Mia. Okay, deep down he knew why he'd done it. He'd wanted to kiss her from the first moment that he'd met her. Plus, he'd been thinking about it since arriving in the Void.

Still, he was too tired to think and had just acted on instinct. If he had been thinking, he would have known it wasn't a good idea. They were in the lion's den, in a mess so big that he honestly didn't know how or if they could ever get out of it.

He was still powerless, and she couldn't return them to Earth or take them out of this realm. They could be stuck there, indefinitely.

This was not the time to let their guard down.

But feeling the rush of energy pulsing from her, he took the kiss deeper. The taste of her was like a drug. He wanted more. Needed more.

The longer he tasted her, the more powerful he felt. Lying her back on the bed, he slanted his lips over hers as he covered her smaller body with his own.

Her fingers dug into his shoulders, into his hair, pulling, holding him. Even the scrape of her nails on his skin, the little sounds of pleasure escaping her lips each time he dove his tongue into her mouth, were addictive.

"Please," she said softly when he trailed kisses down her neck. "Lucas, I need you," she said, as she arched for him.

"Tell me this is real," he demanded as he nudged the shoulder of the sundress that she was wearing down, exposing more of her soft skin to his view and touch.

"It's real." She sighed and wrapped her legs around his hips.

He looked at her under him. Her dark hair was fanned over the bed, her eyes glued to his own. "You've said that to me before." He waited. "Prove it."

"Do I need to pinch you again?" she said with a smile.

"It's too good to be real," he said, running a fingertip over her collarbone, slowly tracing the line. He watched her pulse jump at his touch right there and counted the beats for a moment. "You're too good to be real."

"Do you say that to all the girls?" She cupped his face with her hands. "I'm real. We're really in Atlantis." She pulled him down until he was a breath away. "Whatever happened to you out there did a number on you."

He nodded. "Time and reality were skewed. Still..." He trailed a fingertip over her lips. "This, this is real." He leaned the rest of the way down and kissed her briefly before pulling back again. Then he was lifting the dress up, trailing his fingertips up her legs. "You're perfection." He practically groaned it.

She arched for him. When he nudged her legs open so that he could explore her further with his fingertips, she smiled up at him and then pulled him down until their lips met again.

The Void

"Touch me," she whispered against his mouth.

He wanted to go slow. Wished more than anything they had all the time in the world. Instead, the need to have her, to take her, outweighed everything. Especially since she tasted and felt so damned good.

He ran his hands up her thighs and nudged the silk panties she was wearing aside. Finding her wet for him, he played with her clit, rubbing it until she jerked her hips against his hand.

"More?" he asked against her skin.

"More," she purred.

When he finally plunged a finger deep into her pussy, she cried out and dug her fingernails into his shoulder.

Feeling her body pulse around him had him wanting more than he'd ever wanted before. Seeing her body respond to his touch was the most exciting thing he'd ever witnessed.

Which scared him for some reason. That knowledge was like a bucket of ice water being poured on his entire body. Inside and out.

He looked down at her. She practically glowed as she came down from the high of the orgasm.

She opened her eyes and looked up at him, then tried to pull him further over her, but he stilled and shook his head.

"As much as I want to explore the rest of this, I think we have some things we need to figure out. And while I hate to admit it, I can barely keep my eyes open. I need sleep soon," he said, trying to convince her. What he needed was time to think. Time to get himself back under control.

She smiled slowly and then nodded. She sat up as he shifted away from her. He watched her pull her dress back into place, covering the skin he'd just tasted.

He turned away and closed his eyes as he tried to get himself back under control.

"I can tell you're tired," she said when he yawned. "The good news is…" She shifted so that they were both sitting beside one another again, her clothes back neatly in place. "You haven't far to go for your own bed."

"Oh?" he asked. He could hardly keep his eyes open at this point. In other circumstances, he knew he'd spend the entire night making love to her. But after fighting through the Kri, and stuffing himself with the meal, he was dog tired.

"It's through there," she pointed to another door across the room.

"Good to know." He turned to her, not wanting to move. "We could…" He pulled her close to him. "Snuggle?"

She laughed. "Something tells me you're not a snuggler."

"I am," he countered. "With the right person." He leaned over and placed a kiss on her shoulder. "And right now, you're the right person. But maybe we should talk some more, since we may not have time tomorrow."

"Would some coffee help keep you awake for a while?" she suggested.

He groaned. "I'd kill for—"

"An espresso?" She held up her hand and a cup appeared.

"How did you know?" he asked, walking over and taking the cup from her. He took a sip of the drink. It was exactly like he ordered at his favorite coffee shop by his apartment.

"I've worked at a coffee shop for the past few years. I can spot the type." She shifted until she sat with her back against the headboard, then she produced a mug for herself.

He sat next to her on the other side of the bed and got

comfortable as well while they sipped their coffees. "Okay, you first."

"My family is from here. Hundreds of thousands of years ago, they fled this place and traveled to Earth. There is a library in a cave somewhere in the mountains with the Li's family history dating back before the Shang dynasty in China. Actually, our records pre-date that by a few hundred years. Each and every member of the Li family has been accounted for. The moment I was given the djinn gift, I became aware of all the djinn in my family before me."

Lucas held up his hand to stop her, then set his empty mug down. He had a hundred questions but asked the first one that had popped into his head.

"Given? I thought you were born into it?"

She shook her head. "I was six when my great-uncle Bai passed and gave me the gift. It was supposed to go to my brother, Lei. He died before he could receive the gift."

"I'm sorry." He frowned over at her. "Why you? Why not someone else in the family?"

"Bloodlines." She shrugged and set her own empty mug down. "The elders have always determined who will hold the gifts. They determined that my family's bloodline was the purest."

"Meaning?" he asked, shifting and lying down on her bed a little.

Mia chuckled and mimicked his move by lying down facing him. "I'm not inbred, if that's what you're thinking."

He chuckled. "The thought hadn't crossed my mind." He rested his head in his hands. "Go on," he said and then yawned.

"Anyway, not long after I arrived this time, I was visited by Feng, the first djinn. My ancestor. I can't even calculate to what extent she is my great-great-great... whatever. Or how many generations there were between her and my ancestors when they left this place. What I do know is..." She turned a little more towards him and lowered her voice. "Feng warned me that these people are the reason my ancestors left. That they seek to bind me here somehow. I think that's why I can't leave here."

Lucas's eyebrows shot up.

"Bind?"

She shrugged. "So far, this city and everyone in it has been given into my control and under my protection by two... goddesses? I don't really know what they were. All I know is that they told me I'd see them again and that they wouldn't know me. That it was my duty to remind them who they were the next time I saw them. Then they..." She raised her hands towards the ceiling. "Poof, disappeared into stardust."

He was silent for a moment. "Jain and Proteus warned me that a great war is coming. They said that you and I are the only ones who can stop it."

"Who are Jain and Proteus? And who are we supposed to fight?"

"Jain and Proteus brought me here. They're... well, monsters really." He chuckled softly. "I'll describe them to you in great detail another time. As for whoever we're supposed to fight..." He shrugged. "If they're anything like the Kri, than we're in serious trouble. They or it, whatever, kicked my butt back there." He groaned and shifted to pull her closer to him, wrapping his arms around her waist. "I never saw the creature's true form, since..." A shiver raced through him when he remembered how it had taken Mia's form. "Never mind. But I doubt we'd be able to win anything at this point. We're so unprepared."

The Void

Mia was quiet for a moment. "How are we supposed to do anything without your powers?"

Yawning, he stretched and pulled her completely into his arms, shifting them both until they were spooning.

"Tomorrow we'll figure that out," he said with another yawn.

"I thought you were going to stay in your own bed?" she teased.

He smiled into her hair, enjoying the smell of her, the feel of her body next to his.

"I never said that. You did. I like it right here where I am." He fell instantly asleep.

When he woke, there were three women standing over the bed, looking down at them with curiosity.

He groaned, thankful that he and Mia were still fully clothed, even if they were still holding one another.

Mia jolted awake, sitting straight up. Seeing the women there, she sighed.

"Morning," she said to the woman cheerfully.

"The day has started," the women said together.

"Yes, I can see that." Mia glanced out the window. "We'll be down soon."

One of the women started to talk. "We must dress—"

"I can dress myself today. Thank you," Mia interrupted.

The women looked at him.

"I can dress myself," he said with a chuckle. "Thanks."

The women glanced at Mia one last time before leaving.

"Ugh." Mia plopped down again on the bed. "I forgot to tell you that there is no personal space here."

He rolled over and looked down at her. "Sleep well?"

She smiled up at him, her eyes running over his face. "Yes, and I'd wager you did too."

His hand moved to her shoulder, and he started making

small circles with his fingertips. "I did." He shifted closer. "We could always pick up where we left off last night, now that we're both rested."

She turned her body into his, lifting her hands into his hair. "What did you have in mind?"

Before he could answer, there was a knock on her door and Beth walked in.

"Morning," Beth said cheerfully, not stopping even after she noticed them on the bed together. "I have the morning schedule, for both of you." She set a tray down on the table by the door. "You're both to meet the general after the morning meal."

"The general?" they both said in unison as they sat up.

"I didn't know there was a general," Mia told him.

"Well, we shouldn't keep him waiting then." He jumped off the bed when he realized that the woman wasn't going to leave them alone.

Beth held up her hands, stopping him. "You'll need to be properly dressed to meet him." She glanced down at his clothes. "There are appropriate clothes waiting in your rooms. As well as servants to help you dress." Beth waved her hands towards his rooms.

He glanced at Mia, who just shrugged in response.

Then Beth clapped her hands and the servants that had been in there earlier walked in, holding a new dress for Mia.

When he walked into his room, there were two men waiting for him and strange clothes laid out on the bed.

For the next half hour, he was basically man-handled. The two men dressed him, shaved him, did his hair, and even put his socks and shoes on for him.

Whenever he tried to tell them he could handle something on his own, he was given a strange look until he shut his mouth and took the offered help.

The Void

Then he was shown back into the dining hall they'd eaten in the previous night. Mia was already there, sitting at the same table.

"That was fun," he said when he sat next to her. "You could have warned me."

She was smiling at him. "How does one warn someone that they're about to be dressed like a child? Still, you look good in this style of clothing," she pointed out after running her eyes over him. "Still just as dangerous and sexy looking." She winked at him.

He groaned. "Can't you..." He waved his hands like she did when she conjured up something. "And put me back in my own clothes?"

"Nope, when in Rome," she pointed out. "Or in this case, Atlantis."

He shrugged as a younger girl stepped up and poured their drinks.

This was the youngest person in the realm, the one Mia had talked about. He wanted to ask the girl questions, but Mia stopped him.

"I've tried talking to her and others," she said softly after the girl left. "Most people either can't speak English or won't talk to me." She shrugged. "I'm thinking it's the first. After all, my ancestors didn't just drop into the United States and speak perfect English. They came from here. And when I try speaking Mandarin..."

"You speak Mandarin?" he asked.

"Of course I do," she said in a perfect accent.

"Impressive," he replied in the language, causing her eyebrows to jerk up.

"A man of many talents," she said.

"My family has business all over the world. I know six different languages."

She smiled. "I know ten, including a dead one."

He nodded in defeat. "What do you think this general wants to meet with us about?"

"I suppose it's to discuss the coming war between light and dark?" Mia answered with a shrug. "We'd better eat so we can disappoint him and tell him we have no clue how to fight, let alone win."

Chapter Seven

After the meal in the hall, she and Lucas were shown into a large room in the lower floors of the building.

It was strange, there was an entire city, yet this was the only building people lived in. She had yet to go into any of the other buildings that surrounded them. Were they just empty shells?

Something about the city just didn't feel right. It was as if they were on the set of a movie and nothing but this one building was real.

While they waited for the general, Lucas leaned closer to her.

"There's something strange about this place. I can't put my finger on it," he whispered.

"I was thinking the same thing. I mean, why are there only a couple hundred people and why do they all live in this building?"

"They do?" he asked, sounding surprised.

Before she could answer, a man who appeared to be in his early forties walked in. He was without a doubt the most muscular man she had ever seen. He was followed by six other men, just as impressively built.

The man's eyes ran over her slowly, then Lucas. Instantly, she could tell he wasn't impressed with them.

Without speaking to them, he moved further into the room and started barking orders in a different language to the men.

"I guess that proves that only a handful of people here speak English," Lucas said to her quietly.

The general jerked his head towards them and looked at Lucas as if he was shocked that he would speak while he was.

Lucas's eyebrows shot up in question and in challenge.

She wanted to remind him that he didn't have his strength or ability not to be injured, but she was too afraid to talk, lest she gain the general's attention. Instead, she nudged Lucas with her elbow when the general turned and continued to speak to his men.

It wasn't until she focused that she started to understand what he was saying.

"Your team will need to work extra to get the job done. I expect your men to see to it that there aren't any more disturbances," he barked at one man, who nodded and then quickly rushed from the room.

Then the general turned to another man. "I want you to double your men on the front gate." He pointed to another. "Take some of your men and have them patrol the southern walls as well." Then he waved them both off.

Once they were alone with him in the room, Mia stepped forward and, in the same language, said,

"General, we can see that you're busy. Maybe we should conduct this meeting another time?"

The general's eyes narrowed, then he glanced over to

The Void

Lucas, who nodded as if understanding the man's silent question about whether he too understood the old dialect of Mandarin.

Surprisingly, the general's next words were in English.

"We've been instructed to speak the new tongue around you," he said, motioning to them both. "No one said you knew our language," he continued in broken English.

"No one asked," Mia replied.

The general's eyes narrowed, then he sighed. "Sit." He motioned to some chairs, then walked over and sat down behind a large desk.

She and Lucas sat down.

"You're the djinn?" he asked Mia.

She nodded. "Mia. You're the general?"

"Tibbo," the man answered, then he looked at Lucas. "You?"

"Lucas. And I'm with her." Lucas motioned towards Mia.

"Has she fulfilled the second prophecy?" he asked them.

Mia looked at Lucas, who shrugged at her.

"Maybe you can enlighten us about just what the prophecies are. And how many of them there are," Mia asked.

The general leaned back, crossing his arms over his chest.

"The first, you would come, followed by your chosen companion. The second, you would restore what was taken from him." He motioned to Lucas. "The third, you would fight in the great battle between light and dark and restore this realm to what it once was, before the great darkening."

"The great darkening?" she and Lucas said at the same time.

The general leaned forward. "What have you seen of our great city?"

Mia tilted her head. "There are no children. Only about a hundred or so people. No one leaves or comes."

The general nodded. "Children have become myths, as has there being anything beyond the walls."

"How do you..." Lucas started. "I mean, you are all here. How is it that you exist without children?"

"We have always been," the general answered with a frown.

There was a pause in the conversation.

"Just how old are you?" Mia asked, leaning forward.

The general frowned. "Old? We do not count. We have always been. Since the day Fa Li left this realm, outside of our reach."

"Fa Li?" Mia gasped, then looked at Lucas. "My ancestor who escaped this place."

"Escaped?" The general's voice boomed as he stood up. "She fled, only taking with her those she had created. The rest of us, those that remained, were forced into this..."—he motioned around them—"darkness."

"Just how are we supposed to win against the darkness?" Lucas asked.

"That is not for us to know," he answered. "I have my troops ready for the coming battle. Everyone has been moved into this building for their own safety. We are all now under your protection." The general nodded. "You will let me know if there is anything you need of us. Until then, it is important that you stick close. I would suggest not leaving this tower."

"Why? What is the threat?" Lucas asked.

"Darkness comes," the general answered. "And you

The Void

must be the light that consumes it," he said to Mia. Then he stood up and walked out of the room.

More than an hour later, she and Lucas sat in her rooms. Well, he sat while she paced.

"Why me?" she asked, turning to march across the room once more.

"According to everyone here, because you're the djinn," he answered. "First steps first, how about we figure out how it is you're supposed to give me my powers back."

She stopped pacing. "Good idea." She tilted her head. "How do we do that?"

He frowned. "You mentioned there was a cave somewhere with your family's history in it. Maybe there's something in there that can help us?"

"I tried to go there, before, when I first came here," she answered with a frown. "I couldn't."

"But you said it yourself. In the past few days, since officially taking over here, your powers have grown. Maybe you can go there now?" he suggested.

She nodded. "It's worth a try." She walked over to him as Lucas stood up. "Hold on to me." She wrapped her arms around him and thought of the cave.

Mia knew the instant it worked. The air around them changed. The smell of old leather books, a slight hint of damp cave and dirt engulfed them.

"Wow," Lucas said, then whistled. "This place is... huge."

She smiled. "I did it." She did a little dance of celebration around Lucas, who laughed at her moves.

"This is a cave?" Lucas asked, turning around a few times.

"Yup," she smiled, fully happy with herself.

"Mia," he said, taking her shoulders in his hands. "This

isn't a cave. This is..." He frowned and looked around. "A cathedral carved out of rocks."

She shrugged. "I did mention that all of the Li family history is here." She glanced around the huge library where she'd spent so much time in her childhood.

She'd brought them to the main section of the cave. There were more than a hundred smaller rooms scattered throughout the cave, each one filled with scrolls or books.

When she was young, after she'd come into her powers, she'd been asked to zap new furniture here or bring a bunch of family members so they could read or study.

She'd never really paid much attention, since she had been just a kid. The first few years of visiting this place, she had enjoyed exploring all the rooms. She'd gotten lost several times.

"I was thinking it would take us a few hours to find what we are looking for. We'll be lucky to find it in a lifetime," Lucas said.

"Oh, but you have the added benefit of being with me." She wiggled her eyebrows and then held out her hand and waited. "Let me try something." She concentrated.

Lucas frowned at her. "What are you doing?"

"Shh, just... wait for it." She smiled when she felt a slight pull.

They waited a moment and just when Lucas opened his mouth to talk again, a giant leather-bound book the size of a coffee table flew towards her.

She squealed in surprise at the size of the thing, and then quickly did her best to catch it against her chest.

"Okay, I thought it would be smaller," she managed when he helped her set it down on a table, one she had helped bring to this realm and had drawn or studied at many times over the years. "Somewhere in here is our answer." She waved at the book.

"Can you just..."—he flicked his wrist—"find it?"

"Nope," she said after trying. "I think we have to do this part the old-fashioned way."

Lucas lifted the heavy cover and frowned down at the text.

"It's Sumerian," she said over his shoulder. She looked up at him and smiled. "Stand back." She pulled a chair closer and started reading while Lucas looked over her shoulder.

Several hours later, the table was littered with empty coffee cups, plates, and potato chip bags, the same ones she had always enjoyed when studying for school. Her eyes and her head hurt, and she was pretty sure the answers to their questions were nowhere inside this damned book.

"I need a break." She stood up and stretched her arms over her head.

During the past few hours, Lucas had taken to strolling around the library and looking around.

Currently, he was sitting in another chair, reading a different book. Now he looked up at her.

"Okay." He closed the book and set it down. "What do you have in mind?" he asked, standing up himself.

She glanced around then smiled. "I left something the last time I was here." She walked over to an old chest and opened it, then laughed as she pulled out her old Nintendo Switch. "Wanna see if I can beat my old score?"

He chuckled and took the game from her hands and set it down. He put his hands on her hips and pulled her closer. "How about we play a different game?" He kissed her.

God. How was it that he could make her melt so quickly?

While his mouth moved over hers, he backed them up until her knees hit the huge leather sofa.

"Sometime soon, you're going to have to explain how all this furniture and stuff got in here," he said against her lips. "For now, I'm just thankful there's a sofa."

She wanted to tell him there was a bedroom of sorts somewhere in the cave. But for now this would do. Besides, she doubted her legs could carry her past a few steps.

Gently, he laid her down on the sofa and covered her body with his while she pulled his shirt over his head.

Desperation had sunk in. She needed him. Had wanted him since the night before. He'd done things to her, made her body react differently than anyone before.

Thankfully, Lucas seemed to match her speed. He hiked up her long dress and pulled it over her head.

His hands moved over her skin, heating it. Her body seemed to come alive on its own, moving with his touch as if he commanded her.

When he sucked her nipples into his mouth, she cried out his name, begging him. To do what, she had no clue. Her only thought was for him not to stop. She wanted him. Needed him.

The moment she pulled his pants off his hips and his erection sprang free, she gripped him. Stroked him.

"My god," he groaned. "Mia." She felt him jerk and move with her guidance.

"My turn," she teased, and then she straddled him and trailed her mouth over his bare chest.

She moved down until she took him fully into her mouth. His hips jerked off the sofa as he fisted his hands in her hair.

"Mia." He growled a warning. Then, before she could react, he reversed their positions.

The Void

"My turn," he said, his eyes narrowing as he looked down at her.

"You already had a—" she started, but she stopped when he bent down and laid his mouth over her pussy.

This time, it was her hands that fisted in his hair.

Using his shoulders, he nudged her legs wide so that he could lap and lick her before sliding a finger into her and causing her world to explode.

"More," he said against her skin. "I'll have it all," he warned as he threw off the last of his clothes. Then Lucas stilled and looked down at her.

"I, um," he groaned. "Care to help me out with some protection? I don't even have my wallet."

She chuckled and then waved her hand and a stack of condoms appeared on the table.

Lucas smiled as he grabbed one.

"Cool tricks," he said as he sheathed himself.

Then she wrapped her legs around his hips and pulled him back down to her.

"This probably isn't a good idea," he said, holding himself rigid.

"It's a great idea." She pulled him down so she could lick his neck. "Don't you dare stop," she said, and bit his shoulder softly.

He chuckled and then kissed her again. "Your wish is my command." He slid slowly into her.

A burst of power mixed with her emotions and exploded in her core. Everything she was was called into question.

How had she never experienced this much before? She was immediately overwhelmed, consumed by... everything.

The way his lips brushed against her bare skin. How his fingertips traced little circles over her.

She could feel his pulse in her soul.

She couldn't have stopped the release that built up inside her even if the world was coming to an end.

"Mia," Lucas growled next to her ear.

"Lucas!" she cried out as they fell together.

She thought she'd imagined the pulse of power that had emanated from her the moment they'd come together. After all, nothing like that had ever happened to her before.

"What was that?" Lucas asked a moment later after he shifted them so that they were resting side by side.

"Hm?" she asked, not opening her eyes.

"The entire room shook," he said, shifting slightly.

"It did?" She opened her eyes and saw the chandelier swaying above them. Then she smiled and laughed. "I've never done that before."

"That was you?" he asked.

"I think it was." She frowned. "It wasn't you, was it?"

He shook his head and smiled at her. "Do you think you'll keep these powers when you return home?"

She frowned and felt her heart skip, then she nudged him away from her and sat up to collect her clothes.

"I'm not sure," she said, feeling strange all of a sudden.

"You are returning home, aren't you?" he asked.

She avoided his gaze and busied herself with dressing. Growing frustrated at the dress, she swiped her hand and changed into a pair of yoga pants and a T-shirt instead.

"Mia." He took her shoulders in his hands and turned her to face him. He'd only pulled on his jeans so far and looked damn sexy with his jet-black hair messy from her fingers.

"I don't know yet." She threw up her hands and marched back to the book and slammed it shut, feeling totally frustrated for some reason. She should be limber and relaxed after the mind-blowing sex they'd just had. "I can't explain it, but I feel like I belong here." She turned around and leaned on the table.

Lucas was frowning at her as he sat on the sofa.

"What if we're trapped here?" he asked.

Her shoulders slumped. "Would it be so bad?"

He stood suddenly and walked over to take her shoulders in his hands.

"Whether you want to believe it or not, something big is coming. Back on Earth. Moros's defeat was just temporary. Doom is coming for us all, in this realm and all others. The only way we can stop it is together, and we can't do that if we're stuck here, especially if I don't have my powers."

Mia felt her shoulders slump as Lucas pulled her closer and hugged her.

"We'll figure this out. One thing at a time." He leaned past her and opened the book again. "First, why don't you conjure up some more coffee and sugary treats so that we can get back to work?"

She knew he was right. For most of her life she'd trained for this. Trained for the possibility that she would be needed. Now, there was no way she was going to hide and let her family down.

She rolled her shoulders and sat back at the table to get back to work.

Chapter Eight

While Mia went back to work with a fresh cup of coffee in hand and a bowl of potato chips and a brownie sitting next to her on the table, he strolled through the large space that she'd described as a cave.

It wasn't a cave. At least none like he'd ever seen before. The ceilings were higher than a football field. The walls were light-colored sandstone, and the light from the huge chandeliers that hung all over the place made it extremely bright in there.

There were six enormous columns shaped like upside-down pyramids that were spaced evenly around the giant main room and held up the ceiling high above them.

There were several narrow pathways that led off in different directions from the main room. The bigger room held the majority of bookcases, which were filled with leather-bound books of all shapes and sizes. Each of the smaller rooms that he'd found were filled with old scrolls. Thousands of them.

There were tons of different pieces of furniture around the various spaces, arranged to allow for comfort while reading. Each piece was unique, very old, and well worn, except for the leather sofa and the table Mia sat at. Both of these items appeared much newer.

While Mia read, he explored the cave some more. If this was really a cave, there must be an entrance. Right? Mia hadn't mentioned there was one, but then again, she wasn't saying much since she was determined to figure out how to give him his abilities back.

He managed to find a long hallway with many rooms jutting in all different directions. He found a bedroom in one of the farthest spaces. It would accommodate one person easily but didn't appear to be very comfortable.

Besides books, there were hundreds and hundreds of antiques littered throughout the caverns. Vases. Artwork. Things that probably would fetch a fair price back on Earth and no doubt had belonged to one of Mia's ancestors at some point.

Was this how her family funded their lives?

Mia had mentioned she'd worked at a coffee shop. She lived in the same apartment complex as Scott had, and he knew firsthand that space in that building was expensive. Besides, the family's house just outside of Atlanta obviously cost a pretty penny to keep up.

She drove a fancy new car. Had a college education. And from what he could tell, before they'd come here, dressed in the highest of fashion.

The longer he explored the space, the more he realized that each room was separated into millennia time frames, with the oldest being the farthest from the main area. When he walked around the bookcases, he realized those in the great room were most likely from the past thousand years.

The Void

When he heard Mia gasp, he rushed to her side to look over her shoulder.

"Did you find something?" he asked.

"It's all here." She pointed to the text.

"How to get my abilities back?" he asked, wishing more than ever that he'd had the forethought to study the dead language.

"I haven't gotten to that part, but..." She glanced up at him. "We're here." She pointed. "Us. This." She motioned around then turned back to the book and slowly talked as she trailed her fingers over the symbols. "How we both came to Kòngbái separately. Me being sent by the three fates, exiled here until I make right what my ancestors messed up." She stopped and frowned at the pages. "Make things right, it says." She shook her head and continued. "How you came here, your long trip across the desert in chains, dragged by Proteus, the shape-shifter of sand and sea. How you befriended Jain and gained information from her." She paused scanning ahead. "Us coming here to the cave." She pointed and the gasped again. "They even have... that in here." She waved towards the sofa where they had been naked earlier.

"How?" He frowned, wondering if she was joking with him.

Mia stood suddenly and scanned ahead. Then she slammed the book close.

"What?" He frowned.

Her eyes were huge as she turned to him, shaking her head. "I... we can't read any more." She looked like she was going to throw up.

"Why not?" He moved to open the book again, and she stopped him.

"A warning. Stop reading now or your fates will be

twisted and forever parted and all will be destroyed," she said. "No, seriously, stop reading this now, Mia. It said those exact words," she added with a shiver.

Then she took a deep breath. With a flick of her wrist, she sent the book away. It disappeared silently into the darkness of the cave.

He wanted to rush after it, to see if he could figure out their next move himself, but she stopped him.

"Try shifting," she said suddenly, crossing her arms over her chest.

"What?" He frowned at her.

She nodded with her head. "Try it."

He sighed and stood back, then focused. When nothing happened, she moved forward, slowly lifting her arms to circle around his neck. She lifted on her toes, brushed her lips across his.

He lost himself in the kiss. The feeling of her next to him.

"Now try," she purred as she stepped back.

Without thinking about it, he morphed until his hellhound form and hovered high over her.

When he took this form, all of his senses were heightened. He could smell the fading scent of the sex they'd just had feet away on the sofa. The age of the books and scrolls mixed with the ink and animal hide used to keep the Li's family history alive.

He could smell fresh rain, sand, trees, and... he stilled. Lifting his nose to the air, he let out a low growl. Someone else was near. They were just outside the cave, as if searching for the entrance. He could smell the frustration. The anger. The slight magic they held.

It was almost like Mia's but... different somehow.

The Void

"Lucas?" Mia asked, glancing over her shoulder. "What is it?"

"Someone's out there." He sent the thoughts into her mind. Then he placed his large body between the stranger's smell and Mia.

"Easy," she said softly. "No one can enter the cave except a djinn." She held onto him. "We'd better get back to the city." With one swipe of her hand, their mess from the day disappeared. "Come on," she said, frowning at him. "Turn back. I'd hate to explain to anyone why I brought a dog into the city."

"I'm not a dog." He growled, baring his teeth to her, which only made her smile bigger. When he shifted back, he took her hand in his. "You're sure no one else can enter this place?" he asked, looking off towards the scents that he could no longer smell now that he wasn't in his animal form.

"I'm sure. There's a reason you couldn't find the exit today." She smiled up at him, then lifted on her toes and kissed him.

With a whooshing sound, they were back in her rooms in the city.

"We've been gone for hours," she said with a yawn. "I'm sure it's supper time."

"After all that junk food, you're still hungry?" he joked.

She nudged him. "I did work up an appetite. Besides, they only eat two meals around here."

"They do?" he frowned, feeling his own stomach growl. What he wanted was a greasy cheeseburger and a large plate of fries. But he knew whatever he'd get would be a far cry from it. The last meal had consisted mainly of vegetables. He doubted they even ate meat. Did they even have cows?

"Yes," she finally answered. She took his hand and started out of the room. While they made their way back downstairs to the dining hall, she filled him in on what the book had said about how he had gotten his powers back.

That them coming together was the key.

"I guess sex is the cure to everything," he joked as they stopped just outside the dining room.

He had been too preoccupied before now to try flying, but since they had returned to the city, he could tell his strength and other abilities were back already.

"It wasn't just sex." She rolled her eyes and playfully slapped his shoulder. "It was us coming together. There, in the cave. That returned your powers," Mia whispered as they walked.

"Why?"

She shrugged. "It didn't say. It just said..." She frowned and avoided his eyes. "With us coming together it would return what was hidden."

He figured there was more to it, since it had taken her a while to read that part, but they were walking into the crowded dining hall and he realized she probably didn't want to talk any further about it.

They ate their dinner of more vegetables, fruits, and berries while discussing as little about what had just happened as possible. Beth hovered around them and, for the first time since their arrival, the general sat at the same table as them.

He was curious why Mia didn't let anyone else in on the fact that he now had all his abilities back. Until they had more time to talk about it, he figured he'd play along and keep that information to himself as well.

After the meal, the general asked them to follow him for a private meeting.

The Void

It shocked him a little to see the space on the top of the building, the massive open courtyard that held what Mia described as her throne.

Why the general brought them up there was a mystery, until they stood at the edge of the building and looked out.

"See those fires?" The General pointed over the city and towards the mountains. "They just showed up tonight."

They both looked to where he motioned. Since the evening meal was served after dark each night, it was easy to spot several hundred small fires along the hillsides surrounding the lake that circled the city.

"Who are they?" Mia asked.

The general motioned to a small telescope sitting by the wall.

When they looked through it, all they could see was darkness and the fires.

"There are creatures who live outside these walls. Who inhabit the lands. They have never bothered us nor do we bother them," the general said. "These new beings who have come are abominations. Foul beasts that have no right to the land they consume. They kill everything in their path. They destroy all."

Lucas felt his gut twist. Was the general talking about creatures like Proteus and Jain being slaughtered? Sure, Proteus had chained and dragged him through the desert, but he'd been unharmed. The last thing Lucas wanted was for either of them to be hurt.

"What exactly do you mean by that?" Mia turned on the general.

"They have been brought here by darkness," the general continued, as if not seeing Mia's concern.

"The creatures that inhabit the land beyond the walls are being slaughtered even as we speak." The general turned to them. "And the fires grow closer to the walls each night."

"Are the walls of the city secure?" Mia asked.

"As much as they can be," he answered, then he paused and moved over to talk to one of his men, who had rushed up there to find him. "Sorry," he said when he came back. "I must go and see to some things. I didn't mean to worry you, but... time is short. Whatever it is you're destined to do, I'd request it be done soon."

When they were left alone, Lucas turned to Mia, who stared out over the darkness to the fires.

"I can fly out there. See what we're up against?" he offered.

She turned quickly to him, shaking her head. "No."

"Hey." He took her shoulders and pulled her close. "My abilities are restored. I can't be hurt anymore. Remember?"

"Did you get that black eye you were sporting when you arrived here before or after your powers were hidden?" she asked, tilting her head at him.

He shouldn't have confided in her that back on Earth, when he and his sisters had been fighting Moros, the battle had taken a toll on all three of them, even though they all had superhuman strength and resilience to pain and injury.

"Fine. What if I just flew overhead and didn't land?" he offered.

Mia thought for a moment, then pulled back. "Only if you take me."

"No," he answered immediately.

"Hold on." She held up her hands and smiled. "I have an idea." She waved her hand in front of herself and, to his surprise, she vanished. She was completely invisible.

"What the..." He frowned, but seconds later, she was back.

The Void

"You fly, I'll keep us hidden," she offered with a smirk. Then she waved her hand in front of her and changed back into a pair of black pants, a gray T-shirt, and dark sneakers. She tied her hair up in a long ponytail.

He sighed. "Fine, but we're staying very far up." He turned around and tapped his shoulder. "Jump on my back."

She easily jumped on his back piggie-back style. He shifted to hold her close.

"I've never flown before. I mean, at least not like this." She giggled when he stepped towards the banister.

"All you need to do is hang on." He stepped off the building. Wanting to give her a ride, he let them fall a few floors before pushing up into the night sky.

Mia's squeals of delight had him laughing.

"My god, this is such a rush," she said into his ear.

"We can enjoy a few moments before we head out there," he suggested.

"Take me up high. I want to see the city from above." She held on tighter to him.

He took them up more than a mile above the tallest part of the city. Even though it was completely dark, there was enough light from the three moons in the sky to make out the city streets and buildings.

"Son of a... There really isn't a red desert outside the walls," he pointed out.

There, encircling the high walls, was a massive waterway. He could see the place he'd been dropped off and gauged it was less than a hundred feet to the wall and doorway where he'd entered the city.

"It has to be some form of protection put on the city by the guardians," Mia answered. "This place is beautiful. Even at night." She sighed. "It's still strange how few people there are and that they don't have children."

"I've thought about that." He glanced towards the fires. "If they can't have children, and they don't remember when the last child was born, does that mean that the ones that are here are thousands and thousands of years old? I haven't seen anyone older than late forties, I'd wager. The youngest looks about sixteen."

"I'm not sure," Mia said, then she pointed. "Look, that must be the desert we both arrived in. My Void," she said. "I had no idea this lay just beyond the mountains. I'd always been told never to wander far."

"Maybe it was to protect you?" he suggested as he started moving towards the fires.

"Yeah," she said quietly. "I haven't heard from Feng since I arrived."

"You're great-great whatever?" he asked.

"Yeah."

"Maybe she can't talk to you in the city?"

"I guess we'll find out soon. We're about to cross the wall," she pointed out.

The moment they were over the water, Mia gasped and her hold on him tightened.

"Are you okay?" he asked, thinking about turning around.

"Yes," she said, relaxing slightly. "You were right. Feng is talking to me again. She is upset and wants us to go back to the city."

"Do you want to go back?" he asked.

Mia was silent for a moment. "No." She waved her hand and suddenly he couldn't see his arms and hands in front of him. "I want to see what we're up against and why she sounds afraid for me to see what's out there. We're going to keep going," she said firmly. "Let's go."

The Void

Without hesitating, he took off towards the firelight.

Chapter Nine

Mia held on to Lucas tighter while they flew quickly through the chilly night air. She wanted to lean back and enjoy the ride, but Feng was pretty much screaming in her head to return to the safety of the city.

"Leave us alone," she called out finally.

"Is she still bothering you?" Lucas asked over his shoulder.

"Yes. I don't want to talk to her right now. After we find out what we're up against, I'll listen to her."

"You'd better start listening now," Feng hissed directly in her ear, causing Mia to jerk slightly.

Still, Mia didn't respond. Instead, she scanned the hillside as they drew closer to where the fires littered the hillside.

"I'd suggest we not talk from here on out," Lucas suggested softly. "Some creatures have highly sensitive hearing. They may not be able to see us, but that doesn't mean we should let them hear us."

"Right." She nodded.

"Mia, tell your companion to turn around," Feng said, sounding a little more urgent.

Mia shook her head and held onto Lucas a little tighter. They stopped and hovered about half a mile over the first fire and saw dark shadows moving around just outside of the low firelight. It was as if there was someone there, but they just couldn't make out their forms.

Lucas motioned and she felt him turn towards the next fire. This time they both saw it. There, standing close to the flames, directly in the glow of the firelight, was a shadowy figure.

Darkness. It appeared to be made of smoke. It had long clawed legs and arms, which dug into the dirt as it consumed a creature that appeared to be a deer.

The sounds of the beast eating—bones crunching, hide ripping, and blood oozing—made Mia wince.

Lucas turned and moved towards another fire.

More creatures of smoke and sharp claws. Some ate small animals while others just walked around or stood still as if they were asleep upright.

Lucas turned again, and they followed the line of fires high up into the hills. Each fire had more than six creatures gathered around it. Who knew how many more were waiting or hiding in the darkness and shadows.

They had just reached the highest fire when Lucas turned as if to head back towards the city.

She stopped him by tapping his shoulder after seeing movement at the last fire. Real movement. Not a smoke creature. A human figure.

Lucas stopped and she reached up to nudge his head to where she'd noticed a figure dressed in all black.

Lucas shifted, moving them slightly closer.

They must have made a sound because at that moment,

The Void

the figure jerked around and turned directly towards them, as if they were visible.

Seeing the man's face, Mia gasped and almost lost her hold on Lucas's back.

"There!" The dark figure shouted. "In the sky." He pointed directly at them.

The smoke creatures moved to protect the figure, then raised their long clawed hands and started shooting long boney spikes at them. It was almost as if they were shooting their fingers at them.

"Shit." Lucas quickly shot them straight up into the night air.

Mia cried out and held on as Lucas flew so fast that she had to close her eyes as the wind hit her face.

She felt something whiz by her head, heard the sound of air whooshing past them. Felt a slight sting in her thigh. Then there was silence.

"We're out of their reach," Lucas finally said sometime later.

When she opened her eyes again, they were over the water and the city was directly in front of them.

"Stop," she said to Lucas. He stilled, hovering almost a hundred yards above the front gates to the city.

"Why in the hell didn't you tell me my brother was alive?" she barked at Feng.

"What?" Lucas jerked under her.

"Feng!" she screamed. "Why is my brother alive? Why did he just try to kill us?"

"Shit." Lucas sighed. "Seriously? That was your brother?"

Mia nodded.

"Feng?" she asked loudly, wondering if they were too close to the city.

"I tried to warn you," Feng replied.

"How is he alive?" Mia asked her. "Do my parents know?"

"No, child. Once the elders knew what he was, it was decided to remove him from your family. Your parents believe that he died here, at a creature's hand. An accident. That is all they needed to know."

"Wait, what he was?" Mia shook her head. "What is he?"

"Erebus," Feng answered after a moment of silence. "Darkness. Shadow. Destruction. Death to this realm and beyond."

"He's the one that I..." Mia swallowed the lump in her throat. "The one that I'm supposed to fight?" she asked, feeling slightly sick.

"Yes, child. You are djinn. You are light. Goodness. Life. Savior of this realm," Feng replied.

Mia felt tears sting her eyes. "I... thought he was dead."

"It was for the best," Feng answered. "When the time is right, you must fulfill the prophesy."

"What prophesy?" she asked.

"Light must destroy darkness," Feng answered and something told Mia that was the last that she was going to hear from her ancestor.

Mia sagged and tapped Lucas's shoulder. "Let's go. I'll fill you in on what Feng said inside." She sighed and rested her head on Lucas's shoulder as he flew them back to the rooftop where they had left from almost an hour earlier. By the time they got there, her tears soaked the shoulder of Lucas's shirt.

Thankfully, he remained quiet until after they landed. When they were back on the ground, he set her down gently.

The Void

"Think you can..." He touched her shoulder and she realized they were still invisible. With a wave of her hand, they returned to normal. She turned away, trying to hide her tears, but Lucas's arms wrapped around her.

"Hey," he said into her hair. "Talk to me."

"Lei, he's... Feng called him Erebus. Darkness. Doom. Feng said he was removed from my family to protect us. My parents, we were told that he was dead. We mourned him." The words flooded from her. Everything that had happened, how her parents had been told by the elders that Lei had been killed in this realm by a creature when he'd wandered away from the cave during one of their many trips to prepare him to take the djinn powers from their great-uncle Bai."

Lucas held onto her as she then relayed everything Feng had just told her.

When she finally pulled away from him and took a step away from him, she winced and almost fell on her face. The pain in her thigh had been a dull ache compared to the emotional hurt she was feeling. Now it stung so badly that she couldn't walk. Thankfully, Lucas lifted her into his arms and rushed inside.

When he laid her down on her bed, her tears of pain blocked her vision. She didn't care if she was hurt.

Lei was alive. Her brother was alive. Now she was supposed to fight her brother and... what? Kill him?

Lucas moved around the room, gathering clean towels and ripping the pants that she'd changed into for the flight.

When he poured something over the heated skin on her thigh, it stung and she hissed and sat up.

"Here," she said, holding her hand over the cut. Moments later, the wound closed without a scar.

"You could have told me you could do that." He sighed and relaxed back.

Wiping the tears from her eyes, she realized just how worried he'd been that she'd been hurt.

"Hey, I'm okay." She laid her hand on his shoulder.

He sighed and rested his forehead against hers. "I'm sorry about your brother," he said softly.

She shook her head. "I don't want to think about that now." She pulled him down to her lips. "Make me forget everything."

With one quick swoop of her hand, their clothes disappeared.

Lucas chuckled, then she pulled him down over her as her lips covered his.

"I need," she groaned. "Fast." She rushed to straddle him. Her hair fell around his face as she trailed her mouth over him. She wanted to lick every inch of him. To taste his skin.

Lucas remained still while she explored him. His hands moved to her hair, pushing it aside while she lapped at his flat nipples. When they puckered for her, she smiled and moved lower.

"Witch," he groaned when she traced her tongue over his ribs.

"Nope, I'm a djinn," she corrected with a chuckle. "Djinn," she said slowly while she traced her fingers over his length.

The sound Lucas made was close to a growl. "Don't forget what I am," he said, jerking when she cupped him. "Hellhounds don't play games," he warned.

She chuckled and looked up into his eyes. "I'll have you playing soon enough, dog." She took his full length into her mouth, and his hips jerked up as he arched.

The Void

"Mia," he groaned.

"Beg me," she said as she ran her tongue up his length.

"Please," he said, jerking under her. Then he gripped her hips and flipped her until she was underneath him.

"You'll pay for that," he growled in a low tone as he looked down at her. His eyes glowed gold and heated further when he plunged into her.

This time, she was the one who cried out, begging him.

"Together," he said, leaning down and covering her mouth with his. "Together," he said with one finally thrust as her entire world exploded into a million stars.

She would have thought that after the long day that she would sleep like the dead. Instead, she listened to Lucas's deep breathing and replayed everything that Feng had told her.

Replayed the vision of her brother cast in shadow and standing on the side of the rocky hillside.

The man was nothing like the boy she remembered. If it wasn't for the eyes, she wouldn't have known it was Lei. He'd been born with heterochromia, a rare condition. Especially rare in people with Asian heritage.

How many years had she stared into those eyes from all the family photos? She could only vaguely remember the real boy since she'd been so young. But those still images she had memorized.

The sliver of bright blue in Lei's right eye had, at one point, been the sign the elders had needed that he was to be the next djinn.

What had caused them to change their minds? Why was he now... her enemy? Erebus. She remembered learning about all the old stories. After all, her family was one of those myths.

It was strange how history rewrote factual events and

twisted them. Most of the Li family history had at one point been rewritten by others. Now, instead of one of her djinn ancestors accidentally not hiding their powers from someone else, there were stories of various gods from different cultures with the same powers.

Everyone knew of Zeus and his great bolts of lightning instead of Zhi with the ability to shoot fire from his fingertips.

Then there was Harue, with the ability to fly, who became Hermes, who wore shoes with little wings on them.

Vishnu, the Indian god of preservation with her many arms, was Viu, a Li family djinn with the ability to create many copies of herself. She had lent a hand during a great flood in her village.

The list went on and on.

Each culture had stories of the Li family djinn's that had been turned and twisted over time as they had been passed on.

Apparently, even the story of Atlantis. Someone, sometime, had talked about the place where her family had escaped. The lost city. Most of what they had said about the place was true. It appeared to be very advanced, even though they didn't have elevators or flying machines.

There was power and the buildings were much like those in modern-day cities.

Mia wondered if thousands of years from now she would be a myth that would be passed on through generations, the truth twisted and morphed. Would someone spread half-truths about her life?

She glanced up at Lucas, who was blissfully sleeping, and wondered just what role he would have in her future. She would have never picked someone like him to be with.

The Void

He was too... powerful. Too strong. Far too alpha for her liking.

Then again, she'd only dated a couple of men before. None of them would have gone as far as he had to save her.

She felt her heart kick in her chest and tried to deny just how much it meant to her that he had come this far. Traveling to a different world. A whole other plane of existence.

Rolling over, she gently climbed out of bed and walked over to the window. Looking out, she could just make out the dying lights from the fires in the hills.

Touching the glass, she called out in her mind to her brother.

"Lei?" she said silently, wishing he could hear her. "Why?"

Chapter Ten

The following morning after they showered, Lucas followed Mia down to the large dining room.

"Until we know more, let's keep the bit about my brother being alive and, well, evil, to ourselves," she whispered.

He nodded and then stepped inside the large room beside her.

He could tell instantly that something was off. The room was practically empty. Only about half of the normal crowd sat around the room and when they entered, everyone stopped talking and turned to watch them walk up to their table and sit down.

"What's going on?" Mia whispered.

"I have no idea," he replied.

"There you are." Beth rushed up to them. "There was an attack moments ago."

"There was?" Both of them went on guard.

"It was at the outer wall. Thankfully, it wasn't breached but..." Beth started just as the general stormed into the room with a handful of guards on his heels.

"Do you care to tell us the meaning of this?" The general tossed a folded piece of paper in front of Mia. "It was shot over our wall moments ago."

Before she picked it up, she glanced at Lucas and he could tell that she knew it was from her brother before she even opened it.

He leaned closer and read over her shoulder.

"Hello, sister. I'd wager you were surprised at seeing me. I can only imagine what the elders told our parents about the day I disappeared. No doubt they assumed I was dead. I assure you, I'm very much alive. A war is coming to this realm. One that can only be stopped if you agree to meet me, alone, tonight when the three moons are directly overhead. I'll be waiting at the base of the hills. Always, your brother."

Mia narrowed her eyes and quickly folded the message.

"Have you read this?" Mia asked the general.

He nodded quickly. "Is it true?"

Mia stood suddenly, and Lucas stood up beside her.

"For now..." Mia glanced at him. "I need..." She shook her head and tears filled her eyes.

"We need time," he jumped in. He took Mia's hand and practically dragged her from the room.

When they were alone in their rooms again, Mia tossed her brother's letter down on the bed and started pacing.

She stopped, then she waved her hands and what he assumed was a mimosa appeared in her hand. She downed the entire thing in one swallow and then said, "Screw it." When she waved her hand again, a glass of amber liquid appeared and she downed it as well. "Want one?" she asked.

He shook his head. "No, I'm good." He sat down and

The Void

watched her pace and conjure another glass. This one, thankfully, she sipped.

"Shit, what do we do?" she asked as she walked.

"For starters, you shouldn't meet him," he answered easily. "Especially not alone."

She stopped and glared at him. "Duh." She rolled her eyes and he smiled.

"Okay, then we're agreed?" he asked.

She stilled and crossed her arms over her chest. "Although, I can't be responsible for the destruction of the city," she said, biting her bottom lip.

He stood up and walked over to take her shoulders in his hands. "Mia, you aren't."

"Why does he want to meet me?" she asked suddenly.

He shrugged. "There isn't any way that he could take the djinn powers from you is there?"

She frowned. "Not unless I die and..." She closed her eyes. "Maybe there's something in the..." She groaned slightly. "In the cave."

"What about it?" he asked.

Her eyes opened again. "When you were your furry self, you smelled someone trying to get into the cave..."

"You think it was your brother?" he asked. "What does the cave have in it that he would want?"

"Scrolls. The elders are the ones who know how to transfer the djinn powers to the next in line. There's a ceremony and a song. I used to think it was just for show. Maybe there's more to it. There has to be something in there that he wants. Maybe he thinks he can force me to help him get into the cave?" She was frowning again. "If he finds a way and kills me..." She shook her head. "The Lei I knew would never hurt me." She glanced up at him. "We were close. For the short time he was there."

"Okay, so is there any way to take the powers without killing the host?" he asked.

She shrugged. "I think we should go back to the cave."

She ran her hand over herself and changed the long flowing dress into a pair of black pants, a shirt, and shoes. It was much like the outfit she'd worn the night before, only this time she had a black leather jacket on as well. Then she ran her hands over her long hair and sent the locks twisting up into a braid.

"Let's go," she started, but he stopped her.

"Think you can whip us up a coffee and some scones?"

She smiled. A travel mug appeared in her hand, and she handed it to him before another one appeared for herself.

"Scones?" he asked, feeling his stomach growl. "There's this little place down the street from my apartment in New York, Rubio's Bakery. I stop there at least a couple times a week."

"And you look like that?" she pointed out with a smile.

"I hit the gym five times a week just so I can enjoy a scone three times a week." He chuckled.

She tilted her head and frowned. "I've never thought about a specific place before when getting items. It's all fairly new to me." She sighed and waved her hand, then smiled when a bag with the name Rubio's appeared.

Lucas took the bag, opened it, and sighed. "Blueberry. My favorite."

"I like chocolate scones," she said, looking in the bag, then up at him with a nod after seeing several of both flavors in the bag. "Ready?"

He nodded and then wrapped his arms around her.

Once they were in the cave again, she asked, "Do you think I'll get to keep all these extra powers if we return?"

The Void

The fact that she was now thinking about the possibility of returning to Earth had him smiling. He hoped that he had something to do with her changing her mind.

"Maybe. Maybe you just had to learn how to use them. You said yourself that most of your family members who were djinns had multiple powers." He set the bag of pastries down on the table.

Mia was quiet for a moment. "Do you think he's out there?" she asked, nodding. Then she gasped. "The cave. It must be near where we spotted him last night."

He frowned and, without waiting, shifted into his animal form. Instantly, he smelled the air and knew they weren't alone. He smelled the rotting carcasses of the animals the shadow creatures had been devouring the previous night. The scent of burnt bark and trees was just as strong. As was the smell of one human.

"Yes," he sighed. "He's close."

"He can't get in," Mia assured herself and him. "Only djinn can enter." She wrapped her arms around herself. "It's why I always have to go with the elders when they come here."

"How did they get back here after leaving your brother?" Lucas asked as he shifted back to his human form.

"He wasn't djinn yet. No doubt my great-uncle and the elders brought him here and...I guess left him," she said with a frown. "They brought me here several times before I was finally chosen," she explained. "On one of his trips like that, they must have seen something in him..." He watched a shiver race over her.

Then she turned and sat down in a chair and started eating a scone quietly. He joined her and they ate in silence.

"How difficult is it going to be to find out what your

brother wants?" he asked her once they were both done eating.

She shrugged and closed her eyes and held out her hand. "I don't feel the pull I did last time I did this." She dropped her hand. "Guess we do this the old-fashioned way." She stood up and started walking to the first bookshelf.

He joined her in the search, unsure of what he was looking for.

"It'll probably be the oldest thing in here," she said a few moments later.

"Then we're looking in the wrong place," he suggested. "The oldest items in here are in the farthest rooms." He motioned towards the hallway.

She followed him through the maze of hallways and side rooms until they both stepped inside what he figured would have been the first space chosen to house the Li family secrets.

It was much smaller than all the other spaces. The wood cases that held the thousands of scrolls were worn and almost completely covered with cobwebs.

"I've never been in this room before," Mia said as they stepped inside.

The moment she stepped into the room, something shifted. The walls began to shake, the floor jerked under their feet.

He held onto her only to realize she was staring directly ahead of them. Her gaze was locked in place as if she was frozen.

"Welcome, djinn," a soft voice said, echoing.

He turned and gasped when he noticed the new room that had shimmered into being in front of their eyes. The

The Void

space had opened up and was now much larger than the biggest main room in the cave.

Its arched domed ceiling had a large circular hole cut in the highest spot. The ceiling was smooth, as if it had been carved out of solid stone with magic. A bright light shone through the perfect hole in the top.

Bright daylight flooded in, turning the sandstone room a warm golden hue, almost as if the walls themselves were made of the precious metal instead of stone.

At the center, underneath the bright light from the opening, sat a hundred-foot tall golden statue of a woman with long hair. She was sitting down on a massive throne, much like the one for Mia that sat in the rooftop garden. Actually, it appeared as if it was an exact replica.

The dress the statue wore was like the ones Mia had been wearing since her arrival. It was obvious to him that this was Mia's ancestor. The similarities were uncanny.

The light was shining on it, and the gold was so bright it almost blinded him.

"What's a genie without a magic cave?" he said under his breath.

Mia stepped forward. "Feng?" she called out, her voice echoing in the space.

"Yes, you and your companion are welcome here," Feng answered.

"Thanks," he said under his breath. Mia jerked her gaze towards him.

"You can hear her?" she asked.

He smiled and nodded. "Apparently." He shrugged.

"What is this place?" Mia asked.

"My home and my prison," Feng answered.

"Why does my brother want in here?" Mia asked.

"He seeks to destroy this place," Feng answered. "To destroy me."

"Why?" Mia asked, moving forward a few steps.

When she did, Lucas frowned as the hairs on the back of his neck tingled. Reaching out, he stopped her from entering too far. For all he knew, this was only an illusion.

His instincts were usually spot on and so was his gut, and something was telling him they didn't belong here. Not yet, at any rate.

"Isn't it obvious?" Feng replied. "He seeks the power of the djinn. Your power. If he can't have it, destroying me will destroy the power once and for all. You must fight him. You must win," Feng responded.

"How?" Mia asked. "Are you asking me to kill my brother?"

"You must win," Feng answered. "Even now, he is at the entrance and seeking a way inside."

"He can't get inside, can he?" Mia asked.

"Only the power of the djinn can come and go freely," Feng answered. "Soon, when the suns and moons align on this world, it will be time. Only then can the power be taken or received."

Mia turned to him and frowned. "I... remember the elders talking about that now. How everything had to be in alignment. They were talking about the moons and suns on this world?"

"It is the reason every djinn is born and dies here," Feng answered.

"Then just as long as we keep my brother out, we should be okay," Mia said to Lucas.

"No," Feng answered sharply. "He still holds some power. Eventually, he will break through the magic keeping him out. Even now, the barrier weakens."

The Void

"Then show me how to make it stronger," Mia said.

Suddenly the entire room shook.

"It cannot be done. You must destroy him before he grows too powerful."

Mia shook her head. "Not if I don't have to."

Feng was quiet for a moment.

"Go. When you are here, he can sense you," Feng said loudly. "Go now, child. When the time is right, you must come to me and destroy him. Only then will all be revealed."

Once more, the entire room shook, and suddenly they were both standing back in the small room filled with the oldest scrolls.

"That was..." he started.

"Enlightening," Mia finished as she turned to leave the room.

"Interesting," he said quietly, glancing around to make sure they were alone. Then again, neither of them had actually seen Feng. Other than the massive gold statue.

He followed her back out to the main room.

"Has she ever spoken to you before when you've come here over the past years?" Lucas asked her when they were in the large main room.

"No, this trip is the only time. Actually, she's never spoken to me before. It's as if I was out of her reach before. Like how she can't talk to me when I'm in the walls of the city." She glanced around and sighed. "There's nothing else we can learn here. Let's head back to the city."

He took her hand when she held it out for them.

When they were back in their room in the city, she sat down on the edge of the bed.

"Mia, there was something more... something... deceptive about Feng. She was hiding something. I could feel it," he said, trying to convince her.

Mia frowned up at him. "What would she have to hide? She's been dead for thousands and thousands of years."

He shrugged, still feeling the knot in his gut. "I'm not sure, but something in my gut tells me it isn't right," he said under his breath.

Chapter Eleven

"We both know that there are three moons circling this planet and two suns," Mia told Lucas later that evening. "I asked Beth, who was somewhat helpful, when they would next align." She took a sip of her drink, suddenly feeling thirsty after the long conversation she'd had with Beth. "The moons rarely come into alignment. Never with the suns. However, once every ten cycles, which I assume is years, the suns align on the opposite side of the moons. Beth claims there is a man—she called him, Jessup—who has spent his life studying the phenomenon. She says he would know when they are expected to all line up again."

"Great," Lucas said, leaning back in his chair.

He'd finished all his food while she'd bent closer to Beth and had gained as much information as she could. "Did she happen to tell you where we can find this Jessup?"

"She's going to ask him to meet us on the roof garden after supper," Mia answered with a smile as she took a bite of her food. "I told you I could figure it all out before tonight."

"News flash," he whispered with a strained smile. "It's tonight. You only have a few hours before you're supposed to meet your brother, and we haven't even thought of a solid plan yet." He let out a low growl. "At least not one we can agree on."

She set her glass down and turned to him. "If he could smell us a mile up in the sky when we were invisible, then what makes you think he won't know you're in your dog form stalking him from the woods?" she hissed.

"Not a dog," he corrected, causing her to smile. Then he shrugged. "I smell different after I shift."

"You smell like a dog. Just like I do when I shift." She went back to eating. "Something tells me that dogs are not normal around here. Which would send red flags up to my brother."

"Then make me invisible—" he started, but she gave him a look and he stopped.

He was silent while she ate for a while, then shifted closer to her.

"There is one more thing I can try," he whispered.

"What?"

"It would mean that I would need to leave." He glanced around. "Right away if I'm going to make it back in time for the meeting."

"What?" she asked again.

"Jain," he said softly. "She is nature. Her smell is overwhelmingly natural. I could fly out, find her, and ask her to come watch out for you. She must still be close by."

Mia's eyebrows shot up. "Do you think she would do that?"

He shrugged. "She and her brother brought me here on your orders. She didn't harm me in any way. Actually, she

The Void

seemed concerned about my health and about appeasing you."

Mia frowned. "I didn't put out any order to bring you here. By the time I found out you were here, you were less than a day away."

Lucas frowned and shook his head. "Then who gave the order?"

"It must have been Pandora and Elpis," Mia suggested. "Do you think Jain will helps us?"

"I can at least ask. If not, then we'll go with my plan." Before she could argue, he stood up. "I'll meet you on the roof." He leaned down and brushed his lips against hers before leaving.

When Beth came back to the table and told her that Jessup would be waiting for her, she finished her drink and headed up the stairs to the roof.

She didn't know what she had expected Jessup to look like—maybe skinny and frail, like every science nerd she knew back home—but the man that stood in the center of the roof garden looking at the night sky through a rather odd telescope reminded her of Chris Hemsworth.

She was thankful it was a little dark and even more thankful Lucas wasn't there to see her drool a little.

"You're Jessup?" she asked when he turned towards her.

He frowned at her. "I don't speak the new tongue," he said in the old language.

"It's okay, we can talk like this," she replied in same language.

The man relaxed. "Beth said you had a question for me?" He turned back to the machine.

"Do you know when the moons and suns will be in alignment next?" she asked him.

He chuckled, then glanced at her. "Oh, you're serious?"

He frowned. Then he motioned towards the sky. "Tonight. I'd wager in about three hours."

"What?" She frowned and glanced up at the sky. Sure enough, already the three moons were growing closer to one another. "What about the suns?" she asked, glancing around the dark skies.

"They align on the other side." He motioned in the opposite direction. "They will rise and fall briefly, just for the alignment. For roughly half an hour. Then we will have perfect alignment." He smiled at her.

"Why don't the others know of this?" she asked, thinking of why Beth didn't simply tell her that it was tonight.

He shrugged. "It is not what matters to them. We have long shed our beliefs that these patterns are important. I study them as a hobby." He smiled.

Mia felt her stomach roll. "Three hours?" She glanced off to the line of fires in the hills. That's when she was supposed to meet her brother. Was that significant? Did Lei know something she didn't?

Lucas was out there somewhere, right now, and didn't know that tonight meant so much more than they'd thought.

"Is that all?" Jessup asked her, sounding a little annoyed that she was eating up his time.

She nodded and turned to go, but then turned back to him.

"How old are you?" she asked him. She hadn't wanted to ask Beth or the general. But she doubted she would see Jessup again after tonight.

He frowned at her. "Old?"

"How many years have you been here?" she tried.

He shook his head. "Years?"

The Void

She waved her hand. "Cycles? How many sunrises and sunsets have you witnessed?"

"All of them," he answered, as if that would explain it.

She tilted her head. "How many is that?"

He chuckled. "Too many to count."

She tried a different tactic. "How did you come to be here? Where are all the other people who live here?"

"We are all here," he answered easily.

"Where is everyone who lives here?"

"They are all downstairs," he answered with a frown.

"Who built this place?" She motioned to the buildings.

"You did. Djinn. It is why you've come back. To protect your children." He shook his head and then turned back to his machine.

That wasn't helpful, she thought as she walked over to the edge and leaned on the railing.

What was she going to do if Lucas didn't return in time? Was she going to go meet her brother alone?

She and Lucas had argued all day about the meeting. The more she'd thought about it, the more determined she was to see Lei again.

After all, she was a djinn. She had all these new powers. If she wanted, she was pretty sure that she could fly as well. Actually, now was a good time to find out.

She only had three hours left. Three hours. She felt panicked. She had to do something. She needed to reach out to Lucas somehow. Damn, why didn't this world have cell phones yet? She needed to tell him that the alignment was actually happening tonight.

Glancing over her shoulder, she made sure that Jessup was too busy with his machine to pay any attention to her. Then she ducked behind a large tree and, without hesitation, lifted up into the night air.

Her power was growing stronger. She wondered if it had to do with how much time she'd spent in this place. Or was it due to the alignment? After all, Feng had mentioned that all djinns received their powers during the alignment.

Since she was in the sky already, she decided to take a quick look around.

Jessup had said that the djinn had built this city. The way he'd answered, it seemed as if the people that were living there now were the only ones who had ever lived there and possibly had always lived there.

Seeing a rather short building with all its lights off, she set down on its roof and walked inside.

Holding out her hands, she created a soft blue glowing ball to light her way. The rooms were empty. There was a set of circular stairs, much like the one in her building, but everything else appeared to be just for show.

She hit building after building for the next few minutes and all of them were vacant.

Why would someone create a large city and leave it empty? Then again, was it within the djinn power to create immortal people to fill Atlantis?

After the fifth building, she was done looking and needed to talk to Feng. Setting off, she went out to a few feet beyond the city's wall and called out. "Feng?"

"Sister."

She was surprised to hear her brother's voice instead in her head. She thought of returning to the city, but since her brother was nowhere near her, she stilled.

"What?" she answered after a moment.

"I see your power has grown. Our family must be very proud," Lei said.

"Why are you doing this?" she asked.

The Void

"I would think that you of all people would know," Lei answered.

"You're going to destroy the city?" she practically yelled back.

"Not me. Your actions will bring about the doom of this realm. Trust me, sister. Meet with me. Alone."

She shook her head as tears fell down her cheeks. "I loved you."

"I love you," he said softly. "I've been trapped here, alone, fighting for what is to come. Meet me. I'll explain everything face to face."

"You tried to kill me last time."

Her brother was quiet for a moment. "An unfortunate mistake."

"What? That you missed?" she yelled back. "Lei, don't do this. You can't have the djinn powers. I won't give them to you." When her brother didn't respond she added, "You'll have to kill me first." Without waiting for a response, she returned to the safety of the city to wait for Lucas.

She was standing on the rooftop, leaning on the railing and watching the fires grow bigger along the mountains, when Lucas set down next to her almost an hour later.

His hands moved to her shoulders. "I found Jain. She's making her way to your meeting point now. She'll be there. Watching over you. If anything goes wrong, she's to bring you to a safe spot." He leaned in and placed a kiss on her shoulder. "What's wrong?" he asked after turning her around and seeing her tears.

"I talked to my brother," she said, holding onto Lucas. "He's not going to back down."

"How?" Lucas asked.

"I can fly. I just wanted..." She stopped when Lucas tensed. "I only went five feet outside of the city." She leaned back and looked up into Lucas's golden eyes. "I wanted to ask Feng more about why she made this city, these people." She sighed, then gasped when she remembered the important thing she'd found out. "The alignment is tonight." She motioned to the sky.

"Yeah, Jain told me. If she hadn't, I would have noticed it myself." He motioned to the sky.

She'd been too busy wallowing in self-pity to notice how close the three moons were now. Besides that, the sky was growing lighter as the two suns rose together in the opposite direction.

"I'd wager we have about half an hour," Lucas said with a sigh. "Are you ready?"

She nodded. "I know what I have to do." She felt her heart sink.

"Mia." Lucas pulled her closer and took a deep breath. "Whatever happens now—"

"Don't." Her heart and head hurt too much to hear his next words.

"After." Lucas nodded. Then he bent down and kissed her until she felt her toes curl.

When the kiss was over, she shot up silently into the night sky. Her tears blinded her until she reached up and wiped them clear.

Looking down, she saw Lucas shoot off the roof and head in the direction of the outer city wall, where they had agreed he would wait until the meeting was over.

Taking a deep breath, she glanced down at herself and, with the swipe of her hand, changed into what she thought of as a warrior's outfit—black jeans, a skintight black shirt with a leather corset, black ankle boots, and a leather jacket. If she was going to die, she was going to do it in style.

She looked as good as Lucy Liu in *Charlie's Angels*.

The Void

Damn, she should add this outfit to her closet when she returned home.

When she landed a few feet from her brother, she glanced around.

Lei stepped out of the shadows dressed in a long black robe that reminded her a lot of the smoke creatures.

"No evil minions made of smoke tonight?" she asked, feeling her anger rise.

Lei shook his head. "They're around, but for this, it's just us." When he opened his mouth to talk again, she held up her hand to stop him.

"I want to say something first." She took a deep breath when he nodded in agreement. "You were my everything. I spent what little time we had together looking up to you. You were my best friend. I loved you so much. There's still time to stop this. To return home to your family." She watched his eyes fill with anger and a hint of sadness.

"There was never going to be that possibility," Lei said. "It's not in my destiny."

"What is?" She wanted to scream. "Death and destruction of an entire world?"

Lei shrugged. "It's what I've seen since I was born. There's no stopping it."

"Together, we can do it." She made a move towards him, only to come up against something solid. Frowning, she reached up and touched the invisible barrier.

"It's started," Lei said, looking up towards the sky. Directly overhead, the three moons became one. "We haven't much time now," Lei added as he glanced in the opposite direction. "Take me to the cave."

The two suns were almost in position. Their bright lights combined and somehow made a bright narrow beam that was heading directly towards the three aligned moons.

Lei jerked his gaze back towards her. "Bring us to the cave now!" he practically screamed. "It's the only way. Nothing can stop what's coming."

"No!" She shook her head and beat against her invisible prison. "Let me go!"

Two things happened at once. The entire hillside behind Lei started to move at the same time and a large black demi-wolf jumped out of the shadows just behind Mia.

Chapter Twelve

Hearing Mia scream sent a wave of sheer panic through Lucas. He had to act and didn't even think before coming to her rescue.

Of course he had followed her to the meeting. He'd crept as quietly as he could, knowing that Lei would be too consumed with Mia to notice him. Especially in his animal form.

Besides, he'd masked his dog smell, as Mia put it, with help from Jain, who had littered his fur with moss and floral scents.

When he noticed Jain react to Mia's cries, he'd jumped into action as well.

What he hadn't expected was that neither of them would be able to get to her or to Lei. It appeared that both of them were now surrounded by some sort of invisible bubbles.

No matter how hard he tried, he couldn't even make a mark. While his sharp claws scraped against the invisible barrier as he tried desperately to get to Mia, Jain beat against the blockade on the other side. Neither of them was making any progress, nor was Mia, who beat against the inside. He could see that she was desperately trying to get out, as she glared at him with anger in her eyes.

"Try something else," he cried to her in his mind.

"I told you I could handle this," she said back as she shot fireballs at the barrier. They bounced off and fizzled out.

"It's not working," he hissed. "Even Jain can't get to you." He watched as she tried a few different things.

"Is that..." Mia glanced over her shoulder and motioned towards the creature that was desperately trying to break the barrier. "That's Jain?" Mia pointed to her. Then she stilled and yelled at her brother. "Let us go."

"I told you to come alone," Lei said to her.

It was then that Lucas realized that Lei looked just as uncomfortable as Mia was. Whatever was going on, he got the hint that Lei didn't want to be trapped either.

Suddenly, a loud hissing sound echoed and the sphere holding both Mia and Lei started to rise slowly into the night sky.

Lucas watched in horror as the bubble headed right for the bright beam shooting out of the suns and heading towards the moons.

"Stop them," he called to Jain, and changed back into his human form so he could fly up and continue beating against the obstacle. "Let her go!" he yelled at Lei.

"Lei, stop this!" Mia was crying.

Lei shook his head and held out his hands. "I'm sorry, sister." He sighed. "It's too late. Nothing can stop it now."

Lucas beat his fists against the sphere until he felt as if his bones would break.

They were almost high enough in the sky to enter the beam when he stilled.

"Mia," he yelled, getting her attention. She'd been

The Void

trying to fight her way out and was yelling at her brother to let her go. "The cave," he said. "Go to the cave. I'll find you. I'll get to you."

Mia nodded. Just as she vanished, Lei threw himself at her.

Shit. Had this been exactly what Lei had wanted all along? Had they just played directly into his trap?

Immediately after Mia and Lei had disappeared, the sphere vanished.

Setting back down on the ground, he glanced around thinking. Jain moved over to stand next to him.

"What now?" Jain asked him.

"Now I find her with my nose," he growled, and slipped back into his animal form.

Her scent was strong enough that he could easily follow it up through the hills to the point they had seen Lei that first night. He ran as fast as he could, focusing on getting to her.

He hadn't realized Jain was on his heels until the first shadow creature flew out of the darkness towards him. Jain moved faster than he'd believed possible. Her speed easily matched his, which assured him that in that first trip together, when he'd been chained, she'd taken it easy on him.

Jain's long branchy arms reached out and snagged the misty creature out of the pathway in front of him and tossed it aside like it was a doll.

The faster he ran up the hillside path, the more smoke creatures came at them. Each time, however, their attacks were easily blocked by Jain.

"They have killed my family," Jain cried out as they ran through the bones of all the animals the creatures had devoured in the past few nights.

It seemed to take forever for them to reach the peak where they had spotted Lei.

Mia's scent was so strong here that he knew she was close by.

He had to stop when he came up against a large rock barrier. Instantly, he knew that Mia was on the other side of the solid stone wall.

"Here," he told Jain. "She's here." He shifted back into his normal form and started punching the stone with his bare hands.

Jain stepped up and picked up a massive boulder and started helping him.

When more creatures tried to attack, Jain turned and fought them off while he continued to punch the wall.

"Stand back," Jain said, getting his attention.

He moved aside, and she picked up the largest boulder around and threw it at the side of the mountain. The large thing shattered into a million pieces without making a scratch on the blockade. Whatever was stopping them from getting inside, it was obviously made of magic.

Nothing was going to let anyone inside, at least not unless they were djinn.

"There has to be another way inside," Jain said. "I'll look." She quickly disappeared.

Lucas leaned his hands against the stone and closed his eyes. His heart ached at the thought of losing Mia. He'd been a fool. Now he would never be able to tell her just what she had come to mean to him.

He had never experienced as much love as he felt for her. In the short time he had been with her, she had become his entire world.

The ache he felt just thinking about never seeing her again was so overwhelming that it caused him to sway. Now

The Void

he was never going to be able to tell her how he felt. Tell her that he loved her.

Resting his forehead against the cold stone, he begged.

"Mia." He felt his heart break as a tear slipped down his cheek. "I love you," he whispered.

Suddenly, he felt his entire body shift forward and start falling.

He jerked his eyes open and caught himself before he hit the ground. Somehow, he'd passed right through the solid stone wall. Turning around, he realized that the wall was still intact.

He was now standing just inside the massive domed room that he and Mia had been in when they had talked to Feng. Her golden statue was gleaming in the light from the center of the room.

"Mia?" he called out, searching for her.

"You are not needed here," Feng said in his head. He felt his entire body stiffen. Suddenly, he understood.

Feng was the one who they were meant to fight. She was the one who had trapped Mia and Lei and brought them to the cave. She was the one seeking to take Mia's powers and to destroy everything. Lei wasn't the one they were meant to fight against at all.

He glanced around desperately and finally noticed Mia and Lei hovering almost a hundred feet in the air in front of the golden statue of Feng. They were still encased in some sort of invisible restraint and were unmoving. Their arms and legs were stretched out as if held by invisible ropes.

He rushed closer to them, trying to figure out how to fight against something invisible. Something long gone. How did Feng even have power still?

"Why?" Mia asked as tears rolled down her cheeks.

When he moved to just below her, Mia's eyes darted

towards him. He saw surprise and relief flood her face as more tears continued to fall.

"I've been imprisoned here long enough," Feng said calmly. "Only with the combined power of two from my bloodline, including the current djinn, can I become stronger than before and take back what was stolen from me."

The air started circling around the room, exiting through the hole at the top as the sunbeam and moonbeams collided overhead, far up in the night sky.

When they finally touched, a wide blue streak of light heading directly towards the gold statue. Towards Mia and Lei.

"Let Mia go," Lei hissed. "I'm the one you needed."

"No," Mia shouted back at him.

Lei glanced over at Mia. "It was always my destiny," Lei said softly. "It's what the elders saw that day long ago. They saw this moment. The moment of my doom. If I had become djinn, I would have released Feng, Malik al-Ahmar destroyer. She would have drained my powers then gone on to destroy... everything." He turned and smiled at Mia, then glanced over at Lucas briefly. "Take care of my sister."

"Lei!" Mia screamed as Lei tried to break free from his restraints.

"Silence!" Feng's voice boomed in the space as Lei's body was jerked even higher, his arms and legs spreading farther apart. Lei cried out in pain.

"Leave him alone," Mia yelled.

"I'll devour both of you, then turn this world back into what I desire. Mine. For all eternity." Feng laughed.

Mia's body shifted and moved higher, much like Lei's. Both of them were now directly in the beam of light.

Hearing her scream in pain, something snapped deep

The Void

inside Lucas. He'd never felt anything like it before. Even when he'd been fighting Moros with his sisters.

One minute he was standing below the golden statue and the next he was easily twice the size of the massive thing.

A deep growl emanated from his chest. What form that chest was, he couldn't say. This felt different. He felt powerful. Strong. Protective.

"Release them," he growled, shaking the entire cavern.

The air in the room stilled as his head blocked out the light that had been hitting Mia and the statue.

"No!" Feng cried out. "Remove yourself," she screamed.

"Let Mia go," he said again.

"I will have my power and be released, beast. You cannot stop me," Feng cried, and suddenly he felt his hide ripping open in various places on his body.

Still, he held firm and only after almost being tripped by an unseeable force was he able to push the statue out of the way of the light. Then he bit it, scratched it, and pounced on it until it was nothing more than a twisted and scarred piece of shining metal. A large gaping slice slit it right down the middle, leaving a massive hole in the center.

Suddenly, everything went quiet for a split second.

Then both Lei and Mia started falling towards the ground. Lei cried out but Mia rushed over and caught him in the air, then gently set them down on the floor.

"Lucas?" Mia moved towards him with a frown on her face. "Lucas?" she said a little softer. "I'm... we're okay."

He took several deep breaths, then closed his eyes.

A few seconds later, he felt her arms wrap around him.

"Remind me to never get you angry," she said into his chest.

He wrapped his arms around her and blurted out, "I love you."

"What in the hell was that?" Lei asked, backing away from him.

Mia smiled at him as he looked down at his hands.

"That was Cerberus," Mia answered with a chuckle. "For real this time." She turned and wrapped an arm around Lucas's waist. "Not some silly dog."

He chuckled then frowned as he looked off towards the golden tomb of Feng. "Do you think she's gone for good?"

Mia frowned and glanced around. "All of this is still here." She motioned around, then turned to Lei, who was still looking at Lucas as if he was going to grow two more heads again.

"Lei, you said we needed to be in here. Why?" She walked over and took her brother by his shoulders, shaking him from his fear.

Lucas noticed how much alike they were. Mia was a few inches taller than her older brother, but still, he could see the similarities.

Lei glanced at Mia. "The scroll." He glanced around and frowned. "The first written text. What gives djinn the powers. We must find it. If we can't destroy Feng, it must burn."

Mia stilled. "Why?"

"We have to destroy her," Lei answered, no longer giving Lucas his attention.

"Why?" Mia and Lucas asked at the same time.

Lei turned to Mia. "To break the cycle. Feng Li must never be able to control this or any other world again. It's what the elders saw, that day long ago. If she's allowed to gain the djinn powers again and she is released, she will consume everything."

The Void

Just then a soft laughing echoed in the cavern as teal-colored smoke started to seep from the center of the destroyed statue.

Lei shook his head. "You haven't stopped anything," Lei said, glancing up at the beam of light shining in through the opening.

Suddenly, the ground under their feet shook violently.

Feng's laughter grew and filled the space so loudly, that he cupped his hands over his ears.

"Thank you, son of Rhea and Typhon for destroying my tomb and releasing me," Feng said. "It's a pity I didn't get all my powers back. I'll have to make do with what I did get."

Suddenly, that feeling in Lucas's gut grew. He turned and looked at the destroyed golden statue just as the smoke shifted into a woman, a real woman. She walked out of the large gash his enormous claws had caused and headed right towards the blue beam of light.

She wore a long flowing dress, like the many Mia had been wearing. Only the hem of this one was somehow made of smoke, floating inches above the ground of the cave.

"Now, I can join my lover once more." Feng smiled as she stepped into the bright blue beam of light. Lifting her face to the rays, she called out, "Moros, my love, I am free."

Lucas and Mia screamed as the woman shot up into the beam of light and disappeared.

"Shit," Lucas said at the same time Mia did.

Chapter Thirteen

"Did we just really let Moros's lover free from her prison?" Lucas asked for the third time in the past hour. "One that had held her for thousands and thousands and thousands of years?"

"Yes," Mia and Lei answered in unison.

"I didn't know Moros had a lover." Lucas put his head into his hands.

"I didn't either," Mia answered.

The three of them sat in the main library in the caverns. Mia had conjured up some coffee and fried chicken, which she was craving for some reason.

Her powers were still there, but she was feeling very drained, like she'd just run a freaking marathon. And she hated running.

She heard Lucas's stomach growl, but he shook his head each time she offered to get him something to eat.

"So, basically, instead of defeating darkness, we gave it back its girlfriend?" Lucas groaned.

"Lucas," Mia said, tapping him on the arm. She could see he was spiraling. What she wanted to do was talk to him alone about his admission that he loved her. "The city of Atlantis is still standing," she pointed out. "We know that we need Pandora and Elpis to defeat Moros. This is just a setback," she said, trying to cheer him up. Then she held out a chicken leg towards him. "Hungry?"

He shook his head. "What now?" he asked, looking around. "You're not here to destroy anything? What about your shadow creatures?" he asked her brother.

Lei shrugged. "They're the ones who found me, raised me. They're my family." He frowned at Mia. "Without them, I would have died."

Mia felt her stomach roll. "Did the elders abandon you? Are they really the ones who left you here alone?"

Lei shook his head. "No, Feng did that. When I stumbled into the oldest section of the cave on my last trip here with the elders, she saw me and tried to take what powers I did have then. The elders were arguing over what to do with me. They had apparently seen what I would do if I gained the djinn powers. When Feng found out I didn't have the powers yet, she sent me away. I ended up on the other side of this planet where the shadows rule. It took me years to figure out where the cave was. I didn't know about the city until I finally felt the power of the cave. Felt your power inside." He glanced at Mia. "I felt you each time you came here." He smiled. "Even though you were far away, I knew each time you visited."

"I had no idea," Mia said, feeling her eyes fill with tears. "I had always been told never to wonder. I guess because the elders believed you'd wandered away from the cave and had been consumed by a wild animal."

"I don't think any of them knew that Feng had regained some of her powers. I doubted she had them until you came here," Lei said to Mia. Then he turned and motioned to

The Void

Lucas. "You're probably the only creature strong enough to break her out of that... statue."

Lucas groaned and laid his head on the table.

"Hey, don't worry. She had us all fooled. She's been in my ear my entire life," Lei said.

"She has?" Mia asked.

Lei nodded. "She was desperate to figure out how I could help her escape. She knew I had some powers. Every Li family member does when they're here, though nothing as strong as you are now."

"They do?" Mia frowned.

Lei nodded. "When they are here long enough, they start to manifest." He held up his hand and smiled as a few blue sparks flew from his fingertips.

"Nice," Mia smiled, then she frowned. "You should be the one with the djinn abilities."

Lei shook his head. "No, from the looks of it, you're an amazing djinn. I never really wanted the power." Then he glanced at Lucas "And you are... amazing at whatever that was."

Lucas chuckled. "Screwing everything up?"

Mia wrapped her arms around him. "There's no way we would have known," she assured him. Then she gasped when she thought of something. "Do you think Feng was the one blocking me from getting home?" Mia asked them.

Lucas's eyebrows shot up. "Have you tried to go back?"

To be honest, Mia was afraid to try. Their parents were going to flip when they saw Lei.

"I can't go back," Lei said suddenly.

Mia frowned. "Why not?"

He sighed and shook his head. "I can't leave this place. It's... all I've known for most of my life." He motioned around them. "Once you go, I won't be able to get back in here. The shadow creatures are my family," he said again.

"No, your family is back on Earth in Atlanta," Mia pointed out.

Lei shook his head. "I've been gone too long."

"No, trust me, you haven't." Mia took his hand in hers. "Send your friends back to where they came from. We'll say our goodbyes in the city and head home. If we can." She looked towards Lucas, who nodded once.

Lei sighed and then nodded.

Mia stood and pulled her brother up into her arms. "Thank you for trying to sacrifice yourself to save me." Just holding him made her happy. "Our parents are going to flip." She squealed. Then she reached for Lucas's hand and sent the three of them to the spot on the hill just outside the cave.

While Lei was talking to his shadow friends in an odd chattering language, Mia walked over and wrapped her arms around Lucas.

"How did you get inside the cave?" she asked him.

He frowned. "I'm not sure. One minute I was pounding on the stone there." He motioned to a solid wall of rock. "Then I was inside the cave." He shrugged and avoided her eyes.

She tilted her head. "You said you loved me."

He closed his eyes and nodded. "Later." His eyes opened and landed on hers. "We'll talk later."

"I love you, too," she said quickly.

He smiled and pulled her close and kissed her. When he pulled back, he said in a lowered voice, "We can't bring him directly to Atlantis. There's a reason I had to pass through the Kri. We have to bring him to the water's edge. He has to make it to the city gates himself."

The Void

Mia sighed and nodded. She had known that would be the case. It was one of the reasons the people had instantly trusted Lucas, because he'd passed the Kri test. If she just brought Lei into the city... she didn't want to think what would happen.

"Agreed," she said just as Lei turned and started walking towards them.

"I'm ready," Lei said, stopping in front of them.

Mia motioned to the shadow creatures. "They're leaving?"

Lei nodded. "Believe it or not, they're good. They saved me. We only attacked you the other night because I felt your power. I thought it was Feng, somehow. Then they attacked you, Lucas, thinking you were the one who had taken me."

"They've slaughtered my family," Jain said from behind them. Everyone jumped slightly when she appeared. None of them had known she was there until the entire hillside moved. Mia was once again shocked at the creature that had saved Lucas. The sheer size of the being was breathtaking, along with the fact that she appeared to be made out of moss, trees, and dirt.

"Wow," Lei said, standing back. "I thought I'd imagined you."

"Tell your friends to stop eating my family," Jain said again.

Lei frowned and looked around at the bones of the animals his smoke friends had consumed in the past days.

"They have to eat," he said with a shrug.

"There are fish." Jain pointed to the river.

"Not enough in the mountains," Lei said.

"I can arrange that," Jain said. Then she disappeared. It

took her only a minute to return with a pile of fish the size of a truck.

Lei's smoke creatures rushed over and gobbled some of the fish up.

"This will keep them happy as they return," Lei said after the creatures chattered in response to the new food.

"I will assure that they leave my forest safely," Jain said. The smoke creatures scooped up the fish and started to disappear into the trees and Jain followed.

Lei turned towards Lucas. "Ready?"

"There's just one more thing." Lucas stepped forward. "You have to earn your way into Atlantis."

Mia reached over and took her brother's shoulders. They flew until they reached the edge of the water just outside the city.

Lucas spoke up. "To the Aynah, go directly, Kri's visions may cause thee, Hinder not thy path, resolutely, Embrace the journey, ardently."

Lucas turned to her and nodded and they both shot up into the air.

"See you soon, brother," Mia called out to him as they passed the small space between the water's edge and the city.

It took her brother less than an hour to knock on the gates. Lei was, of course, welcomed into the city with cheers.

Since they had fought Feng all night, the morning meal was very welcomed by all. Lei was cleaned and dressed in the standard clothing that all men wore inside the walls. Lucas even changed, and she had donned another dress.

She was looking forward to returning home so she could wear clothes that fit her style better. Not to mention she wanted to eat some of her favorite foods again.

The Void

"What are we going to tell them?" Lucas asked, motioning to the room.

"About us leaving?" she asked and then shrugged. "I'm not sure. We were supposed to save them from the darkness."

"Yeah, and all we did was let an evil djinn loose." Lucas sighed.

"Right." She groaned. "So, I'm not sure. Maybe we should wait a few days?" She could see the worry flash in Lucas's eyes and reached over to touch his arm. "I'm even more determined to leave now. It's just..." She glanced around and sighed. "A calm before the storm."

Lucas nodded. "A few days."

"Besides, I need to figure out what we're going to tell our parents," she whispered as she motioned to where her brother was eating dinner at the end of their table.

They were just finishing their meal when the general rushed in.

"Soldiers, to the walls!" His eyes flashed to Mia and Lucas, and she knew something was wrong.

Lucas jumped up and rushed over to the general.

"What's up?" he asked just as Mia and Lei reached them.

"Darkness comes. It's time for you to fight," he said, then he turned and left.

Lucas looked over at her with a frown, then they both headed towards the stairs at the same time. Lei followed them as they went up the stairs to the rooftop.

It was funny, the entire time she'd been there, not once had she thought about what sort of weapons the soldiers used. She hadn't seen guns or even swords on their hips. Now, however, each soldier they rushed past on the stairs held a strange stick that she supposed could have been some sort of gun or sword.

They were running too fast for her to stop and see them clearly.

When they finally reached the rooftop, all three of them gasped.

In the sky, blocking out both suns, was a beast. Mia didn't want to call it a dragon, but... it looked like a freaking dragon.

It was easily a mile long, its body thin and snake-like, with huge yellow and red scales. It had long black horns on the top of its head that twisted and turned to make a crown of sorts. It flew through the air like a string caught in a strong breeze. Its wings were translucent and reminded her of a dragonfly's wings, fluttering so fast you could hardly see them.

If it wasn't such a terrifying sight, she would have described it as beautiful and fluid.

Suddenly, long streams of yellow and blue lightning bolts flew at it and hit its scales, bouncing off the creature as it flew around the city.

She looked over and saw the general and his men pointing the long sticks at the creature. The lightning was coming from the ends of the sticks.

"Is that a dragon?" Lei gasped beside her.

The creature stopped and looked down at them. A slow smile formed on its black and red lips.

"There you are, dog." A loud hissing sound filled the city. "Did you really think you could get rid of me that quickly? There is no place you can hide that I won't find you."

"It's Moros," Lucas growled, and instantly he shifted into the giant Cerberus. Seeing Lucas with three heads had

The Void

been a shock the first time. Now she was thankful he'd learned how to control the new transformation. They were going to need it if they were going to win. "Get your sister inside, now," Lucas yelled at Lei before he jumped into the air and latched onto the tail of the long serpent dragon as it flew by them.

Even though Lucas had seemed giant as the three-headed dog in Feng's cave, his looked like a puppy next to Moros's dragon.

Mia turned to her brother, who frowned over at her.

"I'm not going inside," she warned him. "But you'd better, just to be safe." She shot up into the air to join Lucas in the fight.

As she went, she shifted out of the long dress and back into what she thought of as her fighting clothes. She also produced the same sword that she had when she spent that first night in the monolith alone.

"Mia, go inside," Lucas growled when she swiped at the side of the beast. Lucas was attacking Moros, trying to bite the creature's throat with one of his three heads.

As she struck out, the dragon laughed and flicked her away like a fly. She crashed through the glass of one of the tall buildings and came to a stop against a stone wall.

It was strange, but looking down at herself, she realized that there wasn't a scratch on her. Shaking the dust and debris off her clothes, she stood up and made her way back to the window she'd just crashed through.

She made it to the opening just as Moros grabbed Lucas with its large claw and held him down against one of the buildings.

Mia watched blood ooze out of one of his mouths as the other two bit out and fought against the dragon.

Something deep inside her shifted at seeing Lucas hurt.

Something primal. Every fiber of her being shook with anger and fear.

She couldn't lose him. She wouldn't. Not like this.

"Let them be," a soft whisper said next to her ear. "He's due a payback."

"Feng!" she screamed and thrashed her sword around, only catching the teal-colored smoke that floated through the air around her.

"I won't permit my lover to harm you if you leave now. Return to your home and live for another day," Feng said as the smoke circled Mia.

"Never," she cried out as her eyes moved back to Lucas, who was struggling even more. Now, two of Cerberus's mouths were bleeding.

"Leave him alone!" she screamed.

"Don't interfere," Feng warned.

"Fuck off," Mia screamed at her, and swiped the colored smoke again. "Show yourself! Or are you a coward?"

It was silent for a moment, then the smoke swirled until Feng appeared in the flesh. She was the same as she had been in the cave. Her ancestor stood in a long flowing dress only five feet away from her.

"You can't stop him. It's his destiny to take everything he wants," she said, motioning towards the fight.

"You're wrong." Mia smiled, remembering what Elpis and Pandora had told her. "It's our destiny to destroy Moros."

"There's only one who can destroy him." Feng smiled.

"Elpis." Mia smiled.

"Only light can destroy darkness," Feng added, taking another step towards her.

"And only a djinn can destroy another." Mia lifted her

The Void

sword. Using all her strength, she thrust out and sent the blade deep into Feng's chest.

Her ancestor looked amused for a moment, then frowned down at the sword imbedded deep in her chest.

"Where did you get this sword, child?" she said softly.

"I didn't recognize it at first, but when I conjured it for a second time, I realized it was the same one your statue held in your hands." Mia smiled. "Which must mean it's important to bind you."

Feng stumbled as the blade slid out of her chest.

A loud roar had Mia turning around just in time to see Moros rip one of Cerberus's heads cleanly off.

"I said, leave him alone!" she shouted, and felt her entire body shake.

Chapter Fourteen

Lucas was trying desperately to just hold on. When he'd fought Moros before, he'd had his sisters by his side and, even then, he had barely gotten away with his life. Now it was just him fighting. Well, if you didn't count the lightning bolts the general and his men were shooting at the creature.

Honestly, he didn't know why they continued doing so. It was obvious it wasn't stopping anything. Actually, he was pretty sure Moros didn't even know they were there.

The moment he'd seen Moros swipe and knock Mia away, he'd lost the upper hand. Seeing her fly through the glass of a building sent a wave of panic through him, and he'd dropped his guard.

Moros had snagged him out of the air and pinned him against a building. No matter what he did, he just couldn't break free.

He felt his skin tear, blood ooze from his mouth. Controlling three heads was a lot harder than he'd thought it would be. The two extra heads he moved much like you would fingers. Then Moros had snapped one off. Lucas had felt as much pain as you'd feel when breaking a finger. Still, he fought.

Then, Moros was gone somehow. He'd been lifted clear up into the sky and was hovering more than half a mile above him. He heard him cry out in pain. Saw the dragon body twist and writhe in agony.

To Lucas's surprise, the long snake-like body twisted until it was tied in knots while still hovering high above the city. Even the general and his men stopped shooting at it.

Lucas shifted back to his normal form and watched as Mia floated towards him surrounded by a bright blue light. Her eyes were focused on the dragon, which was still screaming in pain.

"This is my world," Mia said in a calm voice, which somehow echoed loudly throughout the city. "And you are not welcome in this realm." She held up her hands.

He'd seen her fireball trick a couple of times now, but this time, the ball of flames she shot at Moros was an even brighter silver color. So bright that he had to shield his eyes.

He heard Moros scream in pain. Heard the cheers from the men stationed all around the walls.

When he looked again, the dragon was curled up in a ball of fire and falling towards the city.

Mia raised her hand again and another ball shot towards the massive body, heading right towards the building that housed everyone in the city. This fireball shattering the creature's body into a million shiny silver pieces, like stars. Instead of raining over the city, they rose high up into the night air.

"This isn't over." Moros's voice echoed as a dark smoke floated where the dragon had been. "Soon you won't be able to stop me. My power grows stronger." The last words were nothing more than a whisper in the air.

The Void

Lucas watched as Mia floated towards him. The moment her feet touched the ground in front of him, he engulfed her in a hug.

"Are you all right?" they both said at the same time.

He chuckled. "Wow, that was some show. Why didn't you do that to begin with?"

"You're okay?" she asked, running her hands over his neck. "I saw..."

He smiled. "I didn't lose my head," he assured her. He frowned down at his hand and held it up. Thankfully, he'd lost his ring finger instead of his head in the fight. "Just a finger."

She gasped and then took his bloody palm in her hands. She closed her eyes and gripped his hand tightly.

Watching his finger grow back was... well, really gross. First the bone appeared, followed by the veins, tendons, muscles, and finally the skin.

"Let's hope you never have to do that again," he said, wiggling his new digit.

She hugged him, and suddenly they were very aware of the cheers that surrounded them.

When they landed back on the rooftop next to Lei, who was smiling at them both, everyone had gathered in the garden area.

She ran a hand over herself and Lucas, changing them back into outfits fit for a celebration in Atlantis. She wore a long silver dress with intricate teal gems embedded all over the silk. Her hair was braided in a circle around her head, and she made sure she included her golden crown on top. The sword hung on her side on a thick leather belt. It too was a symbol of her power.

Lucas she put in a black suit that had deep-yellow

accents along his cuffs, waist, and necktie, which matched his eyes perfectly.

Seeing this, the crowd's cheers doubled.

"Aynah! Aynah!" everyone cheered.

"Who is Aynah?" Mia asked Lucas quietly.

Lucas smiled back at her. "You are. Queen of the djinn." He motioned to the throne. Everyone had cleared a path to the golden seat. "You've delivered them from darkness with your light." He nudged her towards the throne, but at the same time, the crowd started pushing Lucas towards the front with her.

Stopping at the base of the stairs, she frowned at the single throne. Turning, she lifted her hands and the cheers stopped just as the general and his men all appeared.

"This battle is won," she said loudly in the old language. "Thanks to the bravery of the general and his men." She motioned to the warriors. Cheers rose up in support of the men. When they died down again, she turned to Lucas. "And to Lucas, Helios, the sun god." More cheers. When the cheering died down, she turned and, with a wave of her hand, a duplicate of her throne appeared next to the original. This one was slightly different, more masculine. Its gems were a deep yellow to match Lucas's eyes. With a smile and a flick of her wrist, she made a golden crown with yellow jewels appear on his head.

"Helios! Helios!" the crowd cheered.

Lucas chuckled and shook his head. "You're sure about this?"

"For now." She took his outstretched hand.

"You're sure you're going to want to go home?" he asked. A crease between his eyebrows appeared.

"Very," she assured him. "But for tonight, let's be royalty."

The Void

He nodded as they climbed the stairs and took their chairs.

After that, a huge celebration kept everyone busy until after the suns sank and the three moons once again rose in the sky.

He'd almost forgotten about his cell phone, but thankfully it had enough power that he could snap a few photos of him, Mia, and Lei, along with the crowd of people dancing and celebrating.

He wished he'd gotten one of Moros in his dragon form.

"What happened to Feng?" he asked as he and Mia made their way back to their rooms. They had just walked Lei to his rooms a few floors below theirs. She'd told him during dinner about Feng attacking her and how the sword she'd conjured up had struck her down.

"I didn't actually watch her die. I believe that this sword"—she tapped the thin metal blade strapped to her side—"was hers. Nothing else I did to her scratched her, but this... did the trick. Before we go back home, I'd like to leave it in the cave."

He nodded in agreement. "Do you think there's anything in your family archives about it? Where it came from? Why it has the power to hurt her?" he asked her as he let them into their rooms.

The lights weren't working and, he spent a second trying to figure out why they were off. Normally, they came on automatically when they stepped into the room and turned off when they stopped moving. He'd figured it was a sensor of some sort.

"I'm far too tired to think about it," she said as she set the sword and her crown down on the table just inside the door.

"These were once my rooms," a voice said from inside the darkened room.

Lucas tensed and shoved Mia behind him, as a bolt of lightning shot towards him. Suddenly, he couldn't move. Every fiber of his body was frozen.

Mia screamed and rushed towards Feng, who was sitting in the chair across the room.

"Enough!" Feng screamed as a burst of smoke engulfed the entire room. Suddenly, they were standing in Feng's hidden cave again. Mia was once more floating a few feet off the ground, frozen in space.

When Lucas tried to jerk himself free to help Mia, Feng turned her eyes towards him.

"Don't bother," Feng said with a chuckle. "You won't move unless I release you."

"Let him go," Mia said.

"You defeated Moros," Feng said in a strained voice, turning back to Mia.

Feng sat slumped on what remained of her gold statue in the corner of the room. Dark blood oozed from her chest. Her hair was tangled and messy, and her dress was torn in several places. She appeared as if she was dying.

"We're just going to have a talk," Feng said, motioning towards Mia.

Mia jerked in the air and then was lowered to the ground until she was kneeling in the dirt across from Feng.

"You defeated me," Feng said with a slight cough. "How? You can't be more powerful than the all-destroying god or the mother of all djinns. I transformed Moros myself into Ismenian Dracon, the greatest destroyer of all realms. Even though you didn't manage to kill Moros himself, you did break through the powerful spell I cast." Feng shifted slightly. Her eyes shot in Lucas's direction. "I now see you

The Void

for what and who you are, Helios, but it wasn't you who defeated us." Her eyes moved back to Mia. "How is it you're so strong?"

Mia smiled. "You've been slumbering for a long time."

"I built this place, built the city, each glass tower rose up from the sand with a flick of my fingers. Every being within the walls came from my willpower." Feng's voice rose. "The rooms you slumber in were mine!" She waved her blood-soaked hand around, splattering droplets everywhere. "I even created the Kri." Her eyes narrowed. "An eternal test to keep out the vermin and allow only those who are truly worthy to enter my great city. " She added with a laugh, "How many have died trying?" She sighed and then leaned back. "When Malik died by my hand, Fa Li rose up against me and tricked me into my golden prison, but not before she somehow sucked all my powers dry. I watched her leave this realm with the beings that she and Malik had created. They escaped the world I had made specifically for them. It took centuries, millennia, for my powers to build back up so that I could summon the djinn in hopes of gaining my powers back. Imagine my luck when the fates dropped you in my lap. Blocking you from leaving was easy enough with what little power I had. Each time you or another djinn visited over the millennia, I grew stronger. What was hard was removing his powers when I felt him arrive." She motioned towards Lucas. "It was so easy to convince you that your brother was the darkness." She chuckled, then coughed. "That brat has been trying to find and break back into the cave his entire life. This time, he came with an army of darklings. Creatures I had created to keep the back side of this world clean of the foul creatures that were here before. The darklings eat... everything." She smiled and Lucas could see blood dripping from her mouth at this point.

Why wouldn't she just die?

"Why do you want to destroy this place?" Mia asked in a calm voice. He suspected she was thinking the same thing he was. Feng was dying. All they had to do was wait her out at this point.

Feng looked down at her hands before answering.

"I need the power. The energy I used to make this world must once more be mine, even if I have to destroy it all. Since the time has passed to drain you of the power that was stolen from me all those years ago, I must retake it from what I built, if I'm going to join my lover. Soon, he'll be strong enough to devour all worlds and every last realm."

"Why?" Mia shook her head. "I've believed my whole life that djinn were good beings. Created to help those in need. Every one of my djinn ancestors has been good."

"I created Fa Li out of boredom. Malik and I needed a toy." She smiled, then scowled. "While I was off creating and destroying worlds with Moros, Malik went and fell in love with the creature. By the time I came back, they had offspring. They had created so many that they had almost filled my great city with their filthy spawn. That was the day I forbid any of my pure creatures from procreating. When I went to destroy Fa Li, somehow she and Malik together were stronger than even I was and overpowered me. In the process Malik was killed just before Fa Li locked me out of my precious city and put me in this prison. That is, until your dog finally released me." She motioned to Lucas.

Mia glanced at him. "Love is a powerful weapon."

Feng glared at Mia. "It's foolishness," Feng hissed. "Soon, I'll destroy you and every single one of Malik and Fa's spawn. I'll hunt them down in every realm they inhabit and wipe them from being."

The Void

"Don't you love Moros?" Mia asked.

Feng laughed. "He is a great lover. One that will get me the power I seek. Once he consumes all the worlds in every realm, I can share in it."

"Such a shame," Mia said, standing up slowly, fighting the invisible hold Feng had on her.

"How is this possible?" Feng cried out. "How are you stronger than I am?"

"Love." Mia smiled as she looked at Lucas. Then with a flick of her hand, he was free from Feng's hold as well.

When Mia turned back to Feng, the sword appeared in her hands. The same sword she'd set down moments ago on the table just inside their room back in the city.

"Stop!" Feng screamed as Mia held the sword to Feng's neck.

"Why should I?" Mia asked. "You've just admitted that you plan on destroying everything."

"We will build it back. We'll eventually need playthings," Feng said with a slight shrug. Then she smiled. "You cannot destroy me. You are good. Besides, if you do, you'll lose everything. Your powers, the ability to travel between your worlds, even your man."

"I won't lose everything." Mia smiled at Lucas, then turned back to Feng. "But I'm not going to destroy you." Feng's eyebrows shot up. "I think Fa Li had the right idea."

Mia lifted the sword high over her head but instead of striking out against Feng, she held it over her. A fireball of gold flames rose from its tip, shooting high into the sky.

Feng screamed. "No! I won't go back. I won't be imprisoned again."

"You will. Maybe a few more millennia of being in your golden prison will make you see the light," Mia said.

The second Mia pointed the sword at Feng, the bolt of

fire rushed toward her and engulfed her and the remains of the golden statue. Then Mia tossed the sword into the fireball. A bright flashing light filled the entire cavern and, seconds later, the room was thrust into darkness.

Lucas fumbled and almost fell before the light finally returned to normal.

"What just happened?" he asked, moving over to Mia, who was standing in front of the golden statue of Feng, holding the sword in her hands once more.

"I just sent my great-great..."—she shrugged—"whatever she was back into the prison that Fa Li made long ago."

"You couldn't kill her?" he said, wrapping his arms around her.

She shook her head. "Even if she wasn't telling the truth about me losing my powers, I couldn't do it." She sighed and rested her head back. "There's always tomorrow, but for now, I just want to go back to our room, shower, and lie down in your arms." She leaned forward and placed a kiss on his lips. "Then, tomorrow, we go home."

He smiled and held onto her. "I like the sound of that." He wanted to spend a lifetime holding her. But the truth was, he knew that once they returned, there was still a war that needed to be fought.

They still needed to defeat Moros once and for all. And to do so, they would have to find Pandora and Elpis. Thankfully, now Mia at least knew what they looked like.

They were both pretty sure that is what they had meant when they'd told her that she would know them. Mia would recognize the physical forms they'd chosen to show her.

Then Mia winced and leaned back from him. "Oh god." She groaned as she rolled her eyes. "You're going to meet my parents."

Chapter Fifteen

Mia allowed the tears to flow down her cheeks as the image of her parents and grandparents holding Lei in their arms blurred.

"Are you okay?" Lucas said, coming up behind her.

She nodded, not trusting her voice.

It had been a full day now since they'd returned to Earth, to her family home outside of Atlanta.

Leaving the Void—or what she now thought of as Kòng-bái, the great city of Atlantis—had been hard.

Before they had left, she'd broken Feng's last hold on the city. The Kri was no more. Now all creatures could come and go if they chose to. Even the Athaki could leave the city if they chose.

Gone, too, was the restriction Feng had put in place about her creations not having children.

Mia didn't know how to lift all the rules Feng had created, but that one small thing she could do. Soon, Atlantis would be filled. Generations from now, they were going to need each and every shiny building and maybe more. This world was no longer a void.

She and Lucas had made promises to return soon and very often. It seemed as if everyone was happy that the darkness of invisible restraints had been finally lifted from them. She could tell instantly that everyone felt different. Instead of living in the one building in the center of the city, several groups of people had already spread out to other buildings before they had left. Two of them, including Jessup, had decided to explore beyond the city walls and had packed up and set out on their own.

She wondered what great things they would discover. What adventures they would have.

"Mia." Her mother waved her towards them, breaking into her thoughts.

Smiling, she walked into the group hug.

"Thank you," Lei said softly, "for not giving up on me." Then Lei shocked her by waving Lucas towards them.

Lucas shook his head, but Mia and Lei pulled him into the hug and laughed when he just stood there, awkwardly.

"If it wasn't for you, we wouldn't be here," Lei said to Lucas.

Mia watched her parents' reaction and then smiled when they wrapped their arms around Lucas as well.

During that first day back on Earth, while her family had traveled from the city, Lucas had locked himself in the room he'd used before they'd left. She'd heard him on the phone a couple times.

When she asked him if everything was all right, he'd informed her that in his absence, thankfully, Scott had been running the business, Forge International.

Now that they were back, everyone in Hidden Creek was expecting them. He informed her that Selene and Scott were happy she was okay.

"They want us to be there in less than a week," Lucas

The Void

said. "I'll need some time, a day or two, to straighten things up in New York, if you're up for the trip?"

She'd grown thrilled about that possibility. She'd been to New York a few times, but the possibility of seeing Lucas's world, where he lived, where he worked, his parents, was exciting.

Since she hadn't shown up for her job at the coffee shop, she doubted she still had it. Then again, now that it was apparent that she'd retained all of her new abilities, she figured she could be persuasive if she really wanted it back. Something told her she didn't.

She and Lucas had yet to talk about their future together. She wondered if Lucas was going to be okay with moving out of New York. Not that she was opposed to moving there, but something told her they were needed more in Georgia. Since returning, even she had felt the draw to the small town of Hidden Creek.

Something was there. Something they needed. Or would need. Whatever it was, she knew that the longer they delayed the trip, the more the danger would build.

When her parents had arrived and seen Lei, her heart had ached at the knowledge of how much of his life they'd missed.

She wished more than anything she could take that pain away, but while they all sat around the dinner table, eating the pizza they'd had delivered, she understood it wasn't possible.

Lei was who he was thanks to the shadow creatures taking him in and raising him. Feng had created them to destroy, yet they had taken him in as one of their own. Her brother talked about them as if they were his family.

She'd even agreed to take Lei back to the other side of Kòngbái so he could visit them whenever he wanted.

She sat next to Lucas while her parents grilled him on his life, everything from his job to his family.

She'd heard how Lucas had been adopted by the older couple, Leif and Leslie Romano. Lucas explained how he'd just recently met his sisters, Selene and Tara. He left out the part that the three of them were triplets and the children of Rhea, the Mother of Gods, and Typhon, the Father of Monsters.

Still, Lucas was smooth enough that by dessert, her parents and grandparents were in love with him themselves.

"My parents freaking love you," she told him when they were alone in her room after everyone had cleaned up and gone to bed.

"Everyone loves me," he said, leaning back in her bed and crossing his arms behind his head.

She laughed. "I didn't. At first." She bounced down on the bed next to him. He'd removed his shirt and pants and was lounging on her bed in his gym shorts and a T-shirt.

She'd changed into her most comfortable pajama shorts and a tank top. It felt so good to be back in her own clothes.

"You were more of a challenge." He smiled at her and pulled her closer to his side. "Your parents seemed super happy to have your brother back."

"I still can't believe he's alive." She sighed. "And so... normal." She shook her head. "I mean, it's not going to take him long to catch up on the world. He was totally into the new games on my tablet."

"What's he going to do now?" Lucas asked her.

"My parents are going to stay here with him until they figure something out. They had filed a death certificate a few years after he went missing. The official report says he was attacked by a bear when they went hiking on the property. It had been close to what the elders had told them

The Void

when they'd returned home without him. Only it wasn't a bear."

She rested her chin on his chest. "We can head to New York tomorrow," she suggested. "Meet your parents?"

He smiled down at her. "They are going to love you." He brushed a strand of her hair away from her eyes. Then he frowned. "Hidden Creek is calling," he said with a sigh. "I can feel it. Moros is close."

She nodded. "We need Pandora and Elpis."

He nodded and closed his eyes. "Why does it feel like we just left the pits of hell and stepped into even hotter flames?"

"Because we have. How long do you think we have?"

He shrugged and pulled her closer. "Days, weeks, months. Whatever we have, at least we'll be together."

Her heart burst with love, and she placed her lips over his. How was she supposed to know just how much he'd come to mean to her. How much what she felt for him would benefit the fight. Was it like this with all the others?

Each person that had gathered in Hidden Creek had in their own way fought to be with the one they were destined to be with. That love made them all stronger.

Lucas had filled her in on how his sister Selene had kept Moros from taking over Scott. Their love was binding, so claiming Scott as her own had released Moros's hold on Scott, his son. It had been old magic. Much like that of Fa Li and Malik al-Ahmar, her true ancestors. Fa Li, who, after her love's death, had left it all behind to start over in a strange new land. To carry on the traditions they saw fit to pass on.

Love. Kindness. Protection.

The Li family had many great stories of all of those things. History was full of the myths of their heroics.

"Mia." Lucas's hands were running slowly over her hips. "How bad would it be if we had sex in a room just down the hallway from your parents, grandparents, and brother?"

She chuckled. "You thought fighting a dragon was bad?" She sighed. "You did say we can leave for New York in the morning, right? If we leave early enough, they may not kill you."

He sighed. "Okay, I'm going to head to my room now." He started to get up but she stopped him by placing her hands on his chest.

"I didn't say we couldn't fool around first. There's plenty we can do that isn't... sex." She wiggled her eyebrows at him and he groaned again.

By morning, she was packed and waiting for the car that would take her and Lucas to the airport. Her parents tried to talk her into staying longer but she wanted to give them time to catch up with Lei.

Saying their goodbyes, she realized that the best thing she could do for them was to keep them all in the dark about the doom hanging over everyone's head. If Moros won, none of this would have mattered. If they won, then maybe someday she would share with them the trials they'd gone through.

"You're quiet," Lucas said as they made their way back towards Atlanta.

"What if this doesn't work?" she asked in a hushed tone so their driver didn't hear.

"This?" Lucas frowned.

"Not... this." She motioned between them. Then she nodded and opened her eyes slightly. "This."

Lucas nodded. "Oh, right." He sighed and looked out the window. "Then we deal with it, I guess." He leaned

The Void

closer to her. "If you'd been up to it, we could have..." He waved his hands like she did each time she conjured something. "Popped to New York."

She chuckled and shook her head. "I wouldn't chance messing that up. Can you imagine appearing in the middle of Times Square?" She rolled her eyes and he chuckled.

"Okay, so, we're supposed to meet my folks for dinner at the restaurant at eight." He glanced at his watch and then at her. "You can still..." He waved his hand over himself. "Change?"

She nodded. "Are we doing fancy?"

"My parents are always fancy," he admitted with a slight groan. "Funny, up until now, I never really cared." He turned towards her and suddenly asked, "How do you feel about relocating?"

Her eyebrows shot up. "To?" she asked, holding her breath.

"Well, temporarily, Hidden Creek. After?" He shrugged. "Wherever. I was up early this morning looking at houses. I found a farmhouse just down the street from my sister's place."

She smiled and relaxed. "I think it's a perfect idea."

She didn't want to let on how her heart soared in her chest at that moment. Being near people with abilities was like breathing air after being trapped in an underwater cave.

Besides, Mia and Selene had gotten along great. She knew that Lucas's sister had grown up keeping everyone at bay. From her own admission, Scott was the only person she'd allowed to get close to her. Until they'd come along.

She was looking forward to seeing Selene and Scott more than Lucas's family.

She had expected fancy, but when she saw his apartment—scratch that, penthouse—she realized just how rich he and his family were. Not that her own family wasn't wealthy. Having a genie in the family did have its perks. Plus, there were the archives and all the cool old stuff that her family had accumulated over the years. All of it was easily fenced to bankroll their needs.

Lucas's penthouse filled the top four stories of one of the tallest buildings along Central Park. These rooms were just as nice as the ones in Atlantis.

They had ridden the elevator up to the top floor and, when the doors slid open, they stepped directly into his front entry area. It reminded her of an entrance to a fancy office, but just past it was a two-story living room with floor-to-ceiling windows that overlooked the park far below.

She stopped and frowned at him. "Just how rich are you?"

He chuckled and shook his head as he tossed down his duffle bag.

"No, seriously?" she asked, trailing behind him. "Gosh." She stopped and looked at a large painting of a single golden dot on a black canvas. "This is so you." She pointed to it.

Lucas glanced over at it and frowned. "Why do you say that?"

She tilted her head and then smiled. "It's the same color as your eyes." She stepped into the large space.

"Feel free to look around. I have to respond to a few emails." He pulled out his laptop and sat down at the kitchen bar.

The impressive kitchen was off to the left and was bigger than her entire apartment. There were French doors leading out to a narrow terrace that held a long table and almost twenty chairs. There were many colorful potted plants lining the railing.

The Void

The inside dining room was rather small but still impressive with a table that sat eight. It already had place mats and settings at each spot, and she wondered vaguely how often he used the space.

All of Lucas's furniture was modern and chic. Actually, everything in the space was modern, down to the kitchen lights and door handles.

There was a circular four-story staircase off to the side of the room with honey-colored wood flooring and glass railings. She stopped at the base of it and looked up all four floors to a massive glass and iron chandelier that hung down all four floors.

"Do you own this or rent?" she called out to him.

"My father owns the building."

"So your rent is cheap?" she said, and he chuckled.

On the opposite side of the living room was a moderate-sized office. Moderate in relation to the rest of the place, at any rate. There was a full-size bathroom between the office and the living room.

Taking the stairs, she stopped at each floor and was more impressed the higher she went.

The first floor up contained a private gym and a small home theater. On the next floor up there were two smaller bedrooms, each with their own ensuite bathroom.

The top floor was reserved for Lucas's room. His bathroom was floor-to-ceiling Italian marble. The showers—yes, there were two of them—were bigger than most bathrooms and had more shower heads than she would know what to do with.

Then there was his bedroom. She vaguely wondered how many women he'd had in that bed. Not that she had anything to worry about. She could feel how strong their bond was and could see it in the way he looked at her.

Seeing a photo on his dresser, she walked over and smiled down at the picture of Lucas with his parents.

She didn't know anything about Leif and Leslie Romano. Seeing their faces before meeting them somehow relaxed her.

"They're going to love you," Lucas said, coming up behind her. His lips brushed the curve of her shoulder, sending a pulse throughout her entire body. "We have a few hours before we're supposed to meet them. We could... find something fun to occupy our time?" He trailed his hands up and down her sides.

She turned easily into his arms and smiled up at him. "Yes, please."

Chapter Sixteen

Lucas couldn't stop himself from wanting Mia. The way she looked at him made him feel... primal. Backing her towards his bed, he yanked at her clothing, needing to feel her skin next to his. Her fingers dug into his skin and when he struggled to remove his shoes, she snapped her fingers and all of his clothes instantly disappeared.

Chuckling, he glanced up at her. "That's one way of getting me naked, I suppose." Then he motioned to her remaining clothes. "Care to help me out?"

She smiled and snapped her fingers again, and her own clothes disappeared.

"It pays to be a djinn." She held out a packet of condoms. "This you'd better put on yourself."

When they moved to the bed and he covered her, slid into her, and kissed her, he knew that he was home. It didn't matter which world or realm they were in, just as long as she was with him.

Almost an hour later he stood in the elevator with her as

they headed down to the restaurant a few floors down from his penthouse.

"You didn't tell me your parents live in the same building as you." She nudged him in the ribs.

"You didn't ask." He pulled her body up tight against his. "Besides, I did say they own the building, remember?" He chuckled.

She was wearing a sleek teal dress, this one far more modern than the dresses she'd worn in Atlantis. It clung to her like a second skin and was low cut, showcasing her prefect breasts.

His hand moved slowly up her hip.

"You know, we could always cancel," he purred next to her ear, and he felt her melting against him.

When she opened her mouth to answer, the elevator doors slid open. His parents stood on the other side, waiting for them.

"Mom, Dad," he said easily. He took Mia's hand and stepped out into the restaurant's waiting area.

"There you are," his father said with a slight smile.

He'd talked to his parents on the long plane trip home and filled them in on the crazy two weeks he'd been MIA.

Since he'd first discovered his abilities, his parents had done nothing but support him. They knew everything about him and the crazy world hidden from everyone else. Still, they loved him and supported him and had never treated him like anything other than their son.

Since the moment they'd been back, he'd felt an urgency building, much like the one he'd felt when he'd realized Scott was going to release Moros. He couldn't explain the connection he had with Moros, but there was one. He was coming. And soon.

After introducing Mia to his parents, they were shuffled

The Void

inside the restaurant, where they were given priority seating, as always.

His parents expected the best of everything. That extended to him and the woman he'd chosen as a mate. Never in all the years that he'd known them had they been pushy about how he lived his life.

When he'd decided to go to school, they'd supported him. When he'd decided to step into the family business, they'd backed him fully.

The moment he'd shown them what he could do, they hadn't judged. Their only requirement had been to hide what he was from others out of fear that somehow he would be injured.

In all cases, they had been perfect parents.

Even now, while the four of them sat around the dinner table, his parents accepted Mia wholeheartedly.

Within the first few minutes of sitting down for dinner, Mia had his parents eating out of her hands. They were laughing at her jokes and hanging on every word she said as she told them a story about her youth.

When the meal was over, he finally worked up the courage to tell them that they were traveling back to Georgia as soon as possible.

His mother instantly looked worried. His father, oddly, looked proud.

"We know it's something you have to do, son," his father said. "We'll keep things running smooth and work out whatever needs to happen here." He shook Lucas's hand.

"Thanks," he said easily.

As they stepped into the elevator to head back up to his place, his mother hugged Mia.

"What was that?" he asked when they were alone in the elevator again.

"Hm?" Mia turned and wrapped her arms around his waist.

"My parents have never liked anyone I brought to dinner before," he admitted. "Not that they're rude people, but they have certainly never reacted the way they did back there."

Mia laughed and looked up at him. "You've never brought a genie home before."

"Right." He smiled.

"What are the plans for tomorrow?" Mia asked when they stepped into the bedroom.

"What do you want to do?" he asked. "Now that my father has pretty much said that he'll fill in for me around the office until I get back, our time is our own."

Mia frowned as she sat down on the edge of the bed. "We should probably head to Hidden Creek."

He nodded as he moved closer to her. "Is that what you want?"

"What I want is to spend the day shopping, eating wonderful food, and maybe seeing a Broadway show." She sighed. "But I know those things can wait."

He pulled her up until he was holding her tight against his chest. "Then that's what we'll do." He glanced towards the glass and the darkness beyond. "Whatever you want," he said, feeling the desire to tell Mia that their time felt limited.

Something in his gut warned him that if they didn't find Pandora and Elpis soon, they would be too late.

"Lucas." Mia leaned back, looking into his eyes. "What?" She tensed. "Tell me."

Closing his eyes, he shook his head. "I...I'm just tired."

"I've seen you tired. This is something else. Don't make

The Void

me hurt you," she warned. "Because you know I can. I took down a dragon and an evil genie."

He chuckled, then motioned for her to sit again. "Something's building. Somehow, Moros and I are... connected. I can feel that he's getting closer."

"Okay, then we head to Hidden Creek tomorrow."

"You're supposed to find Pandora and Elpis," he reminded her.

She smiled and waved her hand at him. "And I will. Whatever we need will be provided for us. It always is. When I was needed, I bumped into Selene and Scott. Everything will work out." She stood and made her way towards him. "Now, I believe you started something in the elevator?" She ran her lips over his jaw as her hands snaked in his pants. "I think it's only fair that you finish."

His body instantly reacted to her touch. Something deep down inside him told him that it always would.

"Mia," he groaned as she started stroking him.

"Yes," she purred, then she leaned up and bit his earlobe.

Had he said she made him primal? It was too soft of a word. The amount of lust that pulsed through him could have set the building on fire.

"Now," he growled. He lifted her up until her legs wrapped around him. "I need you now."

He reached up under her dress and, in one move, tore her silk panties off. Seconds later he was plunging into her right where they stood.

Mia's head arched back as she cried out his name, begging him for more. He ran his mouth over her neck as her nails scraped and clawed at his arms. When he emptied himself into her, he knew that if they survived whatever dangers they faced in the coming days, weeks, or months, he belonged to her forever.

Two days later, they loaded up his car and headed out to Georgia. They had decided to drive to Hidden Creek, since he wasn't sure how long they would be there, and he wanted his own vehicle.

He'd taken Mia shopping the day before and, he had to admit, he'd had fun. She made him laugh more than anyone he'd ever been with before. They'd eaten lunch at one of his favorite cafés, then after grabbing sushi for dinner at a restaurant she knew and suggested, they purchased tickets to a late showing of Hamilton.

He didn't want to tell her that he'd seen the play before. Besides, within the first few minutes, he was so lost in the story again that it didn't matter.

"Want me to take the first shift?" Mia asked after they had loaded all their items in the trunk of his car.

"No, I got this," he assured her as he opened the car door for her.

"I like your car," she said absently. "I would have expected a Lamborghini or a Bentley." She shrugged and slid into the BMW. "You must have rented the one you had at my place," she said after he slid behind the wheel.

He smiled. "I would never own an Aston Martin myself. I'd have far too many speeding tickets. But they are fun to drive."

"This one is a lot roomier too." She leaned back. "Now comes the most serious question of our relationship..."

He glanced at her before pulling out of the parking garage. "What's that?"

"What kind of music do you listen to?" She leaned forward and hit the power button on his radio.

When "Sweet Caroline" started playing, she laughed

The Void

and turned it up. She sang along as he drove them out of the city.

At ten that night, they pulled over just outside of Atlanta to get a hotel room. They didn't want to arrive in Hidden Creek in the middle of the night since the house he'd arranged to rent wouldn't be ready for them until the following day.

The next morning before hitting the road again, they decided to eat breakfast at the diner across the street from their hotel.

He would never in a million years have imagined he'd be perfectly happy sitting in a highway diner eating a very unhealthy and extremely greasy breakfast.

They had just finished their food when the bell above the door chimed. Normally, he wouldn't have given the pretty blonde a second glance, but since Mia was staring at her in shock, he turned back around.

"What?" he asked Mia.

"It's her," she whispered, motioning towards the woman.

"Who?" He frowned back at the woman.

"Pandora."

Chapter Seventeen

Mia couldn't take her eyes off the woman sitting across the diner from them. It was Pandora. Or, rather, a woman identical to her.

This woman was dressed in worn jeans and a college sweatshirt, wore no makeup, and had her long blonde hair tied back in a braid. Still, she was just as beautiful as when she'd seen her before.

Okay, so her skin wasn't glowing with millions of sparkly diamonds and her hair was a few shades darker than it had been when she'd exploded into stars.

"You're sure?" Lucas asked, leaning across the booth to whisper.

"Positive." She nodded without taking her eyes off the woman.

"Okay." Lucas straightened. "What do we do now?"

She shrugged. "I don't know." She frowned and looked back at Lucas. "Can't you go over there and flirt with her or something?"

He laughed so loud, the woman glanced their way. Oh god.

The moment the woman's eyes locked with her own, Mia thought she would recognize her. Instead, she turned away and looked down at the menu.

"Okay, so I don't think she recognizes me," she told Lucas.

"You mentioned they wouldn't," he pointed out.

"Right." She continued to watch the woman while she thought about what they should do.

"You could go over there?" he suggested.

"And say what?" Mia whispered. "Hey, you don't know me, but I'm a djinn from another realm. Where we initially met, your demi-god version told me I'd find you again and it was my job to get you to remember who you are. Then I fought off a dragon and my evil ancestor, the mother of all djinns. My boyfriend, who happens to be Helios, the son of gods, who can morph into Cerberus, and I want to know if you want to return to Hidden Creek, a small town no one has heard of so you can wake Elpis, a goddess who will help us fight off Moros, the god of doom." She said it quickly in one breath, then took a deep breath, feeling slightly light-headed.

Lucas was smiling. "You just called me your boyfriend."

She rolled her eyes. "What are you? Twelve?"

He reached over and took her hand in his. "Whatever we are, I seriously think of us as more than just that."

She felt her heart flutter. But then it jumped in her chest when the woman got up from her chair and headed directly towards them.

"I'm sorry to interrupt," the woman said with a slight frown, "but did I overhear that you are heading to Hidden Creek?"

"We are," Lucas answered smoothly.

The woman bit her bottom lip. "I hate to ask, but can

The Void

I get a ride with you?" Lucas's eyebrows shot up and then he smiled at Mia. "I'm from there and well, my boyfriend..." The woman rolled her eyes. "Well, now he's my ex. He just broke up with me and left me at the hotel. He even took my purse, and I only have ten dollars in my pocket." Lucas and Mia didn't say anything in response, so the woman continued. "I'm Amy, by the way. Amy Reed. My brother Joe owns a liquor store in Hidden Creek. Hidden Creek Wine & Liquor, if you've heard of it. You can look me up. I'm not some crazy woman, I swear. I was going to call him and have him come give me a ride, but..." She shrugged and glanced out the window. "I didn't want to wake him or Liz up this early in the morning since they work late at the store and, well, Liz is pregnant."

"Why don't you have a seat?" Lucas motioned towards the spot next to Mia.

"Thanks," Amy said.

"I swear Ryan normally doesn't do this. Just up and leave me." Amy sighed. "Joe's been warning me about the guy for months. I guess he was right." She sagged in her chair. "Gosh, you two are such a cute couple. What's your names?"

"Mia." Lucas motioned to her. "Lucas."

"Are you just visiting Hidden Creek?" Amy asked easily as she crossed her legs.

"We're... thinking of moving there," Mia admitted.

"I actually know your brother," Lucas said.

"You do?" Mia and Amy said at the same time.

Lucas smiled and nodded. "I met him the last time I was in Hidden Creek." His eyes met Mia's. Of course, he had gone there to fight Moros after she'd been sent to the Void by the three fates.

"Yes, he helped me with... a problem that I had. We rented the house a few miles from their house," Lucas said.

"Oh, cool." Amy relaxed.

For the next half hour, while they waited for Amy's food, they chatted about the town and filled Amy in on where they lived and what each of them did for a living. How they had met, etc. They left out the parts about powers, fighting gods, dragons, and djinns.

Still, by the time they climbed into his car, Mia was pretty sure she and Amy were going to get along great. The only issue was, how was she supposed to wake Pandora up inside of Amy?

The closer they got to town, the more something bubbled deep inside Mia. She hadn't been to the small town before, but she'd heard about it from both Selene and Lucas.

They were a mile out of town when she asked Lucas to pull over.

"What's wrong?" he asked when she jumped out of the car.

She couldn't explain what was happening, only that she felt an urgency. A pull.

"Are you okay?" Amy asked Mia.

"You need to come with me," Mia said, taking Amy's hand. "Trust me."

Amy frowned over at Lucas, who shrugged. "Let's take a walk?" He reached in and grabbed his car keys and the three of them walked through a field.

"Here." Mia stopped frowning. The feeling was gone. No, not gone just... paused. She looked at Lucas. "Wrong time." She glanced up at the sky. "We need to come back."

He nodded.

"What's going on?" Amy asked. "Why are we in the Anderson's field?"

The Void

Lucas turned to her and then did a circle. "Where's the silo?" he asked Amy.

"Gosh, you know about that?" She smiled. Then she turned and pointed. "Just over there. Jacob keeps the entrance locked now. We used to go down there and party all the time in school."

"We will need the others," Lucas told Mia. "For now..." He glanced at his watch. "It's almost lunchtime. I can text them to meet us at the Harvest Moon Family Restaurant." Lucas turned to Amy and smiled. "My sister Tara owns the new place."

"Oh, I'd heard that it opened up a few weeks back. I've been out of town for... a while." She shrugged. "I can walk from here?" Amy suggested when they headed back to the car.

"No, it's okay. I'll text Joe and have him meet us there too," Lucas said, pulling out his phone.

By the time they'd all climbed back into the car, his phone chimed.

"They're heading there now," he said to the car.

"Thanks," Amy said and sat back. She was quiet for the rest of the trip, no doubt worried about what Mia had just done. She was pretty sure she'd just freaked the girl out. How in the hell was she supposed to get Pandora to wake? Was she trapped in Amy? Did Amy already know?

When they pulled into the small town, Mia immediately fell in love with the place. She'd been in a ton of small towns all over the south before. She'd read all the articles about how the group of people she was about to meet for the first time claimed they had powers. Thanks to Lucas, she knew it was all true. That and more.

For the next hour, introductions were made over lunch. Everyone was there.

Xtina and Michael and their daughter, Harper. Xtina was every bit as mysterious and mystical as she'd imagined she would be from Lucas's stories.

Brea and Ethan and their son, Milo, were also there. She knew that Ethan and Michael were twins. Very identical and hunky ones, at that.

Then there was Jess and Jacob and their son Reed. Jacob was Michael and Ethan's older brother, who also happened to be the law in town. The sexy southern kind of law with his uniform on.

There was Joe and Liz, of course, who were happy to see Amy again and very thankful to them for giving her a ride. Joe appeared to be a meathead. You know the kind—full of rippling muscles and totally head over heels in love with Liz, who was indeed very pregnant.

Joleen and the sexy, nerdy Mason came in later, after everyone's food had arrived.

Of course, there was Lucas's sisters and their partners. Tara was the complete opposite of Selene and Lucas with her blonde hair and fair skin. But she was extremely nice. She and Colt, who was obviously ex-military, were busy running around their new restaurant and didn't really have a chance to sit down and talk much.

Selene and Scott were the only two in the large group that Mia actually knew. She could feel their powers each time she met them. The place practically vibrated with the energy.

"We don't close for a few more hours," Tara said when she stopped by their table to refill everyone's waters. "But if you want, we can all meet out at Xtina and Michael's place this evening?"

"That'll do. We want to go check into our rental and

The Void

maybe have a shower and change," Lucas said, glancing at his watch.

"Let's say, eight?" Xtina suggested.

After they finished their food, they all left and went their separate ways.

"That was all... very normal," Mia said when they climbed back into their car.

Lucas chuckled. "As opposed to fighting dragons and shoving genies back into their golden jails in hidden magical caves?"

She smiled. "Yes."

When he pulled off the main road and parked into a driveway just in front of a three-car garage, Mia leaned forward. "This? This is the house you rented for us?"

Lucas nodded. "Yup, it's all ours for as long as we need it." He shut off the car. "I have the door code here." He glanced down at his phone. "Want to go look around?"

"Do I!" She jumped out, then nudged him when he tried to get their bags from the trunk. "Later." She pulled him towards the front door.

The home was a beautiful classic farmhouse. A wide front porch ran along the whole front of the house. On the right side was a porch swing the size of a bed. The other side had four rocking chairs with cushions. Large windows lined the front of the house, both upstairs and on the main floor.

After Lucas unlocked the door, they stepped directly into an entryway. There was a small circular table with two high-back white chairs encircling it. A low hanging circular chandelier hung over the table. All the wood in the house, including the floors, was rustic looking.

Just to the right of this area was the living room. The walls were wood boards painted white and various paintings hung all over the place. There were more than a dozen small circular mirrors on the other wall and a stone fireplace on the back wall.

To the left of the entryway was the kitchen, which had a massive island in the middle, complete with barstools on one side. There was even a window seat that overlooked the front yard. The cabinets and marble countertops were all white, while the stove vent was the classic rustic wood. To the side of that room was the formal dining room.

While Mia rushed from room to room, Lucas followed along.

"You enjoy seeing new places, don't you?" Lucas asked when he followed her into the dining area.

"Yes, I love watching all those home design shows. There's a pool!" Mia exclaimed.

"May I remind you that your parents' place has a pool?" he said as she opened the sliding doors and stepped outside.

"So, I like pools." She chuckled. "And a hot tub." She wiggled her eyebrows.

He moved to grab her but she side-stepped him. "Let's see the bedrooms."

Up the rustic stairs were three bedrooms, each with their own private baths. Whites, grays, and simple wood furniture filled every space.

It was a far cry from how her family decorated. Mia actually loved this style so much more than the clunky and traditional stuff her parents had filled their home with.

"Maybe we can take a dip in the pool before we head out and meet everyone?" Lucas suggested.

"I guess it's a good thing I packed a suit," she said.

He pulled her close and kissed her. "I was thinking we didn't need any."

Epilogue

Once again, he was sitting in Xtina and Michael's living room, which was filled with people of various power and abilities. This time, however, he didn't need persuading to trust any of them.

Mia was the new outsider here. While she filled everyone in on what they had been through in the past two weeks, he sipped the beer Michael had given him.

When Mia got to the part about Pandora being Joe's sister, everyone gasped.

"Amy?" Joe leaned forward in the chair. "My Amy is Pandora?" He shook his head. "How?"

"How can that be?" Xtina asked.

"I'm not sure. All I know is both Pandora and Elpis told me that I would know them and that I would have to remind them of who they are," Mia answered.

"They need to awaken," Xtina said as she took Michael's hand. "Each of us, whether we knew it or not, had slumbered until we needed one another." She looked at Michael, then around the room until her eyes landed on Joe. "Pandora's asleep now. We simply need to wake her up."

"How? By finding her mate?" Mia asked with a shrug. "And I'm responsible for that?"

"Possibly."

"And what will happen then? Will Amy then die or go to sleep? Will I lose my sister?" he asked with a shake of his head.

"How much did you change after finding out about your powers?" Xtina asked him.

Joe frowned at her. "Not at all."

Xtina nodded. "Your sister has always been Pandora. We just need to bring the part of her that's asleep out. Somehow."

"Did she or Elpis mention how to achieve this?" Jessica asked.

Mia shook her head. "Nope, just that I would have to remind them of who they were."

"Okay, so, what? You tell her?" Brea asked.

"No." Mia frowned. "I think we need to go to the silo. When we drove past it today, I got this feeling that I needed to take Amy there."

"Okay, so, we take her there," Jess said, standing up. "Can you call her?"

"No." Mia shook her head. "Not yet. It's... complicated. When the time is right, I'll know," she said with a shake of her head.

"Okay." Jess sat back down. "What happens until then?"

Everyone turned to Lucas as if he had all the answers. The funny thing was, he did.

He glanced down at Mia and smiled. "Now, we train."

Also by Jill Sanders

The Pride Series

Finding Pride

Discovering Pride

Returning Pride

Lasting Pride

Serving Pride

Red Hot Christmas

My Sweet Valentine

Return To Me

Rescue Me

A Pride Christmas

The Secret Series

Secret Seduction

Secret Pleasure

Secret Guardian

Secret Passions

Secret Identity

Secret Sauce

Secret Obsession

Secret Desire

Secret Charm

Secret Santa

The West Series

Loving Lauren

Taming Alex

Holding Haley

Missy's Moment

Breaking Travis

Roping Ryan

Wild Bride

Corey's Catch

Tessa's Turn

Saving Trace

Christmas Holly

Maggie's Match

The Grayton Series

Last Resort

Someday Beach

Rip Current

In Too Deep

Swept Away

High Tide

Sunset Dreams

Lucky Series

Unlucky In Love

Sweet Resolve

Best of Luck

A Little Luck

Christmas Wish

Silver Cove Series

Silver Lining

French Kiss

Happy Accident

Hidden Charm

A Silver Cove Christmas

Sweet Surrender

Second Chances

Dancing on Air

Entangled Series – Paranormal Romance

The Awakening

The Beckoning

The Ascension

The Presence

The Calling

The Chosen

The Beyond

The Void

Haven, Montana Series

Closer to You

Never Let Go

Holding On

Coming Home

The Hard Way

Never Again

Pride Oregon Series

A Dash of Love

My Kind of Love

Season of Love

Tis the Season

Dare to Love

Where I Belong

Because of Love

A Thing Called Love

First Comes Love

Someone to Love

Fools in Love

FindingLove

Christmas Joy

Always My Love

Forever My Love

Searching for Love

Wildflowers Series

Summer Nights

Summer Heat

Summer Secrets

Summer Fling

Summer's End

Summer Wish

Summer Breeze

Summer Ride

Distracted Series

Wake Me

Tame Me

Save Me

Dare Me

Stand Alone Books

Twisted Rock

Hope Harbor

Raven Falls

Angel Bluff

Day Break

Diamonds in the Mud

For a complete list of books:

http://JillSanders.com

About the Author

Jill Sanders is a New York Times, USA Today, and international bestselling author of Sweet Contemporary Romance, Romantic Suspense, Western Romance, and Paranormal Romance novels. With over 90 books in eleven series, translations into several different languages, and audiobooks there's plenty to choose from. Look for Jill's bestselling stories wherever romance books are sold or visit her at jillsanders.com

Jill comes from a large family with six siblings, including an identical twin. She was raised in the Pacific Northwest and later relocated to Colorado for college and a successful IT career before discovering her talent for writing sweet and sexy page-turners. After Colorado, she decided to move south, living in Texas and now making her home along the Emerald Coast of Florida. You will find that the settings of several of her series are inspired by her time spent living in these areas. She has two sons and off-set the testosterone in her house by adopting three furry little ladies that provide her company while she's locked in her writing cave. She enjoys heading to the beach, hiking, swimming, wine-tasting, and pickleball with her husband, and of course writing. If you have read any of her books, you may also notice that there is a love of food, especially sweets! She has been blamed for a few added pounds by her assistant, editor, and fans... donuts or pie anyone?

- facebook.com/JillSandersBooks
- twitter.com/JillMSanders
- amazon.com/Jill-Sanders/e/B009M2NFD6?tag=jillm-com-20
- bookbub.com/authors/jill-sanders
- instagram.com/jillsandersauthor
- tiktok.com/@jillsandersauthor

www.ingramcontent.com/pod-product-compliance
Lightning Source LLC
LaVergne TN
LVHW041809060526
838201LV00046B/1189